TAINTED HEARTS

Garren Michael San Julian

iUniverse, Inc.
New York Lincoln Shanghai

TAINTED HEARTS

All Rights Reserved © 2004 by Garren Michael San Julian

No part of this book may be reproduced or transmitted in any form or by any means, graphic, electronic, or mechanical, including photocopying, recording, taping, or by any information storage retrieval system, without the written permission of the publisher.

iUniverse, Inc.

For information address:
iUniverse, Inc.
2021 Pine Lake Road, Suite 100
Lincoln, NE 68512
www.iuniverse.com

ISBN: 0-595-32513-0 (pbk)
ISBN: 0-595-66618-3 (cloth)

Printed in the United States of America

Contents

Chapter 1   "Beginning of the End" 1
Chapter 2   "Tragic Friends" 7
Chapter 3   "A Year to Remember" 17
Chapter 4   "Acceptance" 25
Chapter 5   "Rollercoaster Ride" 38
Chapter 6   "It Can Happen" 42
Chapter 7   "Deeper and Deeper" 54
Chapter 8   "The Contract" 71
Chapter 9   "Second Thoughts" 79
Chapter 10 "Circle of Life" 86
Chapter 11 "The Thief" 97
Chapter 12 "Discovery" 106
Chapter 13 "Questions" 115
Chapter 14 "Answers" 129
Chapter 15 "End of the Beginning" 138

ACKNOWLEDGEMENTS

I would like to thank all of my family and friends who have supported and encouraged me throughout my journey to create this novel. Thank you to Susan for recommending the Outerbanks of North Carolina where I began writing and falling in love with this story. Thanks to Ken for seeing something different and suggesting the novel's title. It truly is a tale of tainted hearts. Special thanks to my editors and great friends, Sherri and Ralph. Your advice, suggestions, and support mean a great deal to me. To my friend Gracie, thank you for the extra push I needed to see the "light." I have come to count on you more than you know. Daphne, your vision and quick turnaround are very much appreciated. Thank you for the wonderful cover design.

There are many more people I could mention who have taken an interest in me and this novel. I continue to be amazed by this wonderful life and how fortunate I am to have such great people surrounding me. I am truly blessed and I thank you.

To my readers, thank you for selecting this book. Buried within this story is the idea that dreams, no matter how far-fetched you think they are, do come true. After you read the final word but before you put this book down, think about your goals and dreams. Whatever you do, don't give up and don't stop dreaming. Things have a way of working out, especially when you least expect them. You never know what tomorrow will bring.

Lastly, I'd like to dedicate this book to my daughter, Kylie Marie. My overwhelming desire to have my own child formed the basis for this novel. Little did I know that when I created this story seven years ago, I would have you in my life when I was done. I love you and your mommy very much.

CHAPTER 1

"Beginning of the End"

The year was 1997. It was a typical July afternoon in San Francisco—cold and damp. The weather seemed to go hand in hand with a funeral. The roses around the cemetery were in bloom with rich, vivacious colors. Through the patches of fog, the vibrant, blood-red roses stood out. Along side them were other rose bushes laden with golden yellow and snowflake white colors which were comforting to the eye. They seemed to enjoy this type of weather and were so fragrant. One could smell their scent from fifty-feet away. It didn't take much to imagine their beauty on a clear day when the sun shines brightly. A sunny, San Francisco day made it seem like everything was right in the world like children playing, friends laughing, and people enjoying the outdoors. But today there was nothing to smile about, nothing to laugh about, nothing to look forward to, and no one to provide enough comfort to get through the day. The only comfort was the smell of the roses and the freshly cut grass. The grass was a thick, deep green and had just been mowed that morning. If it weren't for the tombstones, the place would have resembled the botanical gardens in Golden Gate Park.

Although some neighborhoods in the city were enjoying the warmth of the sun, Matt was glad it was cool. Under any other circumstance, he would enjoy being out among nature's wonders. But as the mist fell from the white, puffy clouds that rolled in over the hills, Matt couldn't help but be comforted by the cool sensation the mist provided to his face. On occasion, the sun's rays would penetrate through the thin layer of clouds as if God were trying to shed some light on this dreary day. When the light did manage to make it through the layer of clouds that hovered overhead, they reflected off Matt's short, shiny, black hair and his golden brown Hispanic skin.

Matt was the type of person to whom everyone took a liking. There was something in his brooding, dark hazel eyes. He had the most beautiful eyes. There were flecks of gold and light brown along with the emerald green that always displayed how he was feeling. All his friends knew when he had been crying because his eyes became much more green. He always wore a smile that showed off his pearly white teeth and dimples. Although he hated the braces he wore when he was a child, their results paid off as an adult. He was also the type of person who would do anything for a friend. He treated friends like his family and on more than one occasion, he let them borrow money to get out of a predicament, drove them home when they had drunk too much, and surprised them on their birthdays with parties surrounded by all of their close friends. But now, on this day, he didn't display any of that energy; his eyes didn't appear to be as bright; his zest for life appeared to be absent. As he stood there, he couldn't help but think about everything that had transpired. Why was he here? How did it come to this? Why him? He hated funerals, but was accustomed to them. "After a while," he always said, "You tend to numb yourself to death." After all, it was an inevitable event.

Of course, this wasn't an ordinary funeral. He never thought he would be burying his lover. He never imagined that he would have such a short life with Ryan. He always believed they'd be together forever and grow old together. Not until then would they have to worry about saying goodbye to each other. But then life doesn't always happen the way one plans. Matt knew this. He had buried many friends and relatives over the short thirty-six years he had been alive. He felt as if he was dreaming or moreover, having a nightmare. It seemed just like yesterday that his childhood friend Maureen (or as he liked to call her, "Mo") had introduced him to her doctor friend, Ryan Anthony Cavazos. He took a moment to reflect back to that day and their first encounter, five years ago.

The place was Mo's and the occasion was her housewarming. Matt walked into her house and standing by the fireplace was a tall, tanned man with short, sandy-brown hair and round tortoise shell glasses. Something happened to Matt when he saw him. It was as if life had stopped for a brief minute and they were looking at each other through a tunnel, with everyone else in another world. Matt didn't believe in love at first sight, but he couldn't refute what was happening, what he was feeling. As time stood still, Matt heard a familiar voice. Mo had approached him and in her best party attire and attitude, trying so hard to be eloquent said, "Welcome, Matthew Michael Tylo, I'm so glad you could make it. Would you like me to introduce you to him?"

"What are you talking about?" Matt replied.

"Oh, come now Matt, you are so obvious! Has it been that long since you saw a cute man? Oh, wait a minute, I guess it has!" she said laughingly.

"I don't think I was that obvious, was I? Oh, who cares anyway," Matt responded.

"Well, are you going to introduce me to him or not? If you don't, I will!" Matt continued, half-jokingly.

"We both know you're too shy to go up and introduce yourself, so I'll do it. After all, I am the hostess!" Mo stated.

Mo was a fun person with a warm personality who seemed to know how everyone was feeling and was able to console anyone with her words of advice. Of course, there were times when she seemed to know too much and seemed to offer too much advice, but this was rare. Sometimes Matt and Mo wouldn't see eye to eye on things, but for the most part, they were inseparable.

As she approached Ryan and tossed her brown, curly hair which was just below her shoulders, she said, "Ryan, I want you to meet my best friend in the whole wide world, this is Matt. Matt this is Ryan. He's a friend of my doctor, Carol Richardson and is also a doctor."

"Oh really," Matt sprang into the conversation, "Are you a general practitioner or do you specialize?"

"I specialize. Specialize in delivering babies. I'm an obstetrician," Ryan said jokingly.

"Are you kidding?" Matt said thinking Ryan was pulling his leg.

"No. I am an O.B. You can just ask Maureen if you don't believe me," Ryan replied.

"Really, why did you choose that field?" Matt inquired, trying to think of anything to keep the conversation alive.

"You know, I just enjoy bringing new lives into the world. There's nothing greater than that. Besides, I love kids. I tend to think I have a wonderfully blessed job," Ryan replied.

Matt was becoming more and more interested in what Ryan had to say.

"Why not become a pediatrician?"

"I'm not really sure except that my great grandfather was an obstetrician so I guess I wanted to follow in his footsteps."

Thinking back brightened Matt's day, even though it was difficult to find anything to smile about. Today was one of those days no one wants to experience but he faced the reality that he was now standing over Ryan's casket. The tears starting swelling in his eyes as he thought about that first meeting and everything that they had meant to each other.

He thought, "No! I can't break down now, I have to be strong."

As the guests started arriving, Matt stood still and stared at the casket that held his dreams and hopes of happiness. He tried to be strong but he couldn't help the tears from falling. Before long, it seemed as if everyone he and Ryan had ever known was there. As Matt looked around, he saw their friends Peter and Jason who were a couple of clowns who thoroughly enjoyed life and each other. They always acted as if they didn't have a care in the world and simply enjoyed each other's company. That's probably why they had been together for as long as they had. It was nice to see them there, together. Tim and Marc were there and still appeared to be in love with each other after five years together.

"That could have been me and Ryan," Matt thought. It was ironic that they were there; after all, they had met at the same party where Ryan and Matt had met. Matt remembered how the four of them would double-date and how close they became. There were nights when they would stay up until the early morning talking about what they wanted out of life and planning vacations together. It had only been a week ago that they discussed taking a trip to Barcelona, Spain. Ryan's schedule at the hospital prevented him from being able to be as whimsical as the rest of them. As Matt looked at them, Tim winked at him as if to say, "Hang in there." Matt felt the warmth of his tears rolling down his face as his lip began to quiver. Nothing was going to be the same again. Ryan was his whole life and now he was gone.

As Matt composed himself, he looked around to see Cassie, Eric, James, Carol, Diane, Kevin, and Thomas. What fun they all had together. Occasionally they took weekend trips together that allowed them to bond even further. Each of them was good at hosting parties, too, when it was his or her turn. Next to Matt was his mother and to his left were Mr. and Mrs. Cavazos. Standing next to them was their daughter, Emily. Matt continued to look around and noticed that the crowd had grown considerably. He didn't recognize everyone and figured the majority were probably from the hospital where Ryan worked. Just before the priest began his eulogy, Matt noticed a tall woman adorned in a black dress, wearing a black hat with a veil that covered her face. She was standing several feet behind the crowd that had now formed. She appeared to be quite eccentric. Her outfit resembled something that Joan Collins would have worn at a funeral scene as part of her *Dynasty* character, Alexis Morrell Carrington Colby Dexter Rowan. Like everyone there, he knew she was there to support him and to show her love for Ryan. He figured he would meet her at the get-together after the funeral. It was customary to have everyone gather at the house of the deceased or at relatives to pay their respects to the family. Usually only close friends and relatives attended. As the priest continued, Matt had only one thought, "just get through this day." He remembered what his friend Cassie told him just before heading from the mortuary to the cemetery, "The funeral is the worst, after that each day gets better and better, you just have to be strong." He wondered if that was true. He'd been to many funerals but none that shook him to his core like Ryan's passing.

He knew the funeral would be difficult but thought the friends and relatives coming over afterwards would be much more difficult. He knew as soon as his mother, one of his cousins, or one of his and Ryan's friends came up to him, he wouldn't be able to control his emotions and he would start weeping.

The service was beautiful, though. Ryan would have thought so. The priest was reaching the end of the service when he began saying some very interesting words that everyone could relate to rather than just the typical sermon that no one really understands. He talked about when we lose someone like the way Ryan passed, we always question ourselves and ask why? He went on to talk about how we always cry at the loss of the individual when what we should be doing is appreciating and celebrating the time we had with the individual. He continued to discuss how grateful we should be that we had the person in our lives at all. Matt could see people's faces change. Some had smiles on them as they remembered the good times with Ryan. Matt couldn't help but continue to cry as he thought about the wonderful times that they had shared and the fact that he wouldn't be sharing any more of them with him.

The priest looked at Matt and signaled him to place the red rose he had picked to place on Ryan's casket. They were at the end of the burial service. Just as Matt took a step forward to place the rose on Ryan's casket, a loud, shrieking shot rang out. Screams began to fill the air and people were falling to the ground for cover. Everyone was frantically looking around to see where the shots were coming from and if anyone had been hit. Matt felt like everything was moving in slow motion. Had he been hit? He didn't feel any pain and couldn't see any blood. As he looked around, he tried to find his mother and his closest friends. They were all crouched down onto the ground. None of them had been shot. He saw the priest praying as he took cover behind Ryan's casket. He could tell he was mumbling the Lord's Prayer. Matt looked back up to see the rest of the guests. The ones that weren't on the ground were screaming. Chaos was breaking out as they started running to their cars or hiding behind trees to get out of the way of the gun fire. Matt stood up to see if he could find who was responsible or whether it was just a car backfiring. As he looked up and down the hill, he saw something from afar that looked like someone running away but the fog had rolled in, making visibility difficult. As everyone cautiously began standing up, they noticed that the women in black had fallen to the ground and was not moving. Matt could see the darkness of the blood that was splattered all over the green grass. A stream of blood was flowing down the grassy hill. He froze.

The priest, followed by several other guests, ran to her side. As they approached her, Matt could hear them yelling something but couldn't make out what they were saying. His heart was racing so fast the only sound he could hear was that of his heartbeat. He turned away to see if the fog had dissipated in order to see the man he'd seen before but he couldn't. As he looked back at the woman in black, there were several people around her, tending to her, holding her head. Her hat was off and the people looked back at Matt, waiting for his reaction.

CHAPTER 2

"Tragic Friends"

Maureen Marie Farnsworth had long, brown, curly hair with golden highlights. She was somewhat of a chubby little girl but in a way that was cute. She had the most angelic, friendly smile. She hated her new silver braces that sparkled when she smiled. Her mother had been pressured by Maureen's orthodontist to fit her with braces. Her mother hesitated because she was so young but the orthodontist argued that if she got braces now, she would avoid overcrowding and substantial work on her teeth in the future. Maureen's mother finally agreed and insisted on it after two months of trying to get Maureen to agree to it. Her mother even told her about how beautiful she would be when she grew up but that didn't seem to convince Maureen. She finally succumbed to getting them after her mother told her that Audrey Hepburn had braces when she was a child. Maureen's mother hoped this would work, knowing how much Maureen adored Audrey Hepburn and loved *My Fair Lady*. Maureen's hair accentuated her olive skin that looked so smooth. Maureen's little brother, Billy, shared his sister's good looks. She was jealous of the fact that Billy didn't have to wear braces but waited for the day when hers would come off and Billy would have to get his. It was August 30, 1969 and an unusually warm day in San Francisco.

"Maureen Marie, it's going to be a lovely day for your first day back to school dear. Hurry up or you're going to put us behind schedule!" said Maureen's Aunt Catherine as she tried to get Maureen ready for school.

This morning seemed to be more difficult than any other. Maureen finally brought herself into the dining room for her usual Fruit Loops and toast. Aunt

Catherine was always good about preparing some type of pastry for the week. Today, she had prepared cinnamon rolls which looked and smelled divine. The essence of cinnamon traveled all the way up the stairwell and provided the stimulus Maureen needed for this day.

This school day was the hardest for the little eight-year old. It was just two and a half weeks since that dreadful night. She remembered hearing her father argue with her mother over taking her to Sacramento to join them in celebrating her father's landmark contract that he had settled with one of the largest retail stores to build their new stores throughout the valley. The 2.7 million dollar contract was the largest ever signed with Farnsworth & Associates. The gala event was to honor Thomas Farnsworth and to provide an opportunity for all of his associates to meet all the principals of the retail store.

"Maureen's running a small fever and I'm not taking her out," her mother told her father, a stern yet caring man.

"This is an important event and since Billy can't go I was hoping Maureen could go at least," replied her father.

"I'm afraid Maureen may have contracted Billy's chicken pox and I don't want to take any chances," Mary, her mother, responded rather adamantly.

Maureen remembered sitting atop the stairs listening to their conversation that went back and forth, until her father gave in and said, "Fine, I guess you're right, I just thought that this would be exciting for Maureen to experience something so grand and I wanted my family by my side tonight. But I know you are only thinking of her and I'm being selfish, so it's better that she stay at home. Besides, the party will probably last for hours, anyway." The conversation resonated in Maureen's mind every night since then.

Thomas's sister, Catherine lived nearby and had the task of watching the children whenever Thomas and Mary wanted to go out alone or if they had a party to attend. It was rare that they went anywhere without the children, but it allowed Catherine some quality time with her niece and nephew.

The evening was a great success and most enjoyable for Thomas and Mary. As the party started dying down, the Farnsworths made their rounds to say goodbye to everyone.

Paul, one of the new associates with Thomas' firm said, "Mary, you must be very proud of your husband. This is one of the greatest achievements I've ever been witness to and it makes me very proud to be working for Thomas."

Although his comments were appreciated, Mary knew from past parties that Paul was always trying to impress Thomas and if he couldn't or didn't have the opportunity, he'd try to impress Mary.

"Take care Paul, drive safely and I'll see you first thing in the morning on Monday. I'd like for you to work on this project and would like to go over some of the details with you," replied Thomas.

It was just after midnight and the Farnsworths were debating on getting a hotel or driving back to San Francisco.

"Oh honey, the weather is so gorgeous and look at that full moon! Let's just drive back," Mary suggested.

"Okay," said Thomas, "your decision wouldn't have anything to do with your concern over Maureen's temperature would it?"

"You know me too well dear," said Mary.

"I hope so, after twelve years of marriage. You know, I think I love you more at this moment than when we first were married," said a blushing Russell who rarely showed his emotions.

"Thank you. What a wonderful thing to hear, I love you too. More than you'll ever know," said Mary as she grinned.

The Farnsworths headed back to their plush San Francisco home in St. Francis Woods. As the two were enjoying their drive and admiring the full moon that lit up the evening sky, they realized they were just about half way home. Mary reached over and held Thomas' hand that was rested on the middle console and whispered, "I love you." Suddenly, without any notice, Thomas saw a pair of headlights coming directly at him. He tried to swerve but didn't have time. The other driver fell asleep, drove through the flimsy divider which separated the two directions of traffic and hit them head on. Another driver behind the Farnsworths had seen everything and took the next exit to phone for help. It wasn't long before ambulances, fire engines, and the highway patrol were on the scene. The twisted metal on each car had rendered them unrecognizable. The first ones to arrive were the highway patrol. The patrolman knew what was in store for him. The drunk driver had been thrown from the car through his windshield and was lying on the asphalt, choking on his own blood. There was nothing they could do for him and he died shortly thereafter. Thomas Farnsworth died instantaneously and Mary was rushed to the local hospital. After hours of trying to save her life, the emergency room doctor pronounced her dead at 4:12 am.

Maureen remembered being awakened when her Snow White alarm clock read 6:38. Those red numbers would be with her for the rest of her life, as if they were permanently burned into her eyes. She remembered Aunt Catherine waking her up and saying, "Maureen, are you awake? I have something very important to tell you."

She could tell from the look on her aunt's face and the tone of her voice that something was wrong, terribly wrong. She remembers her heart beating louder and louder until she could feel every beat pounding in her throat.

Aunt Catherine continued, as if in slow motion by saying, "your mommy and daddy were in an accident" as tears flowed gracefully down her porcelain cheeks.

"Are they alright?" Maureen managed to get the words out although she thought she knew the answer.

"I'm sorry honey, there both gone."

She remembers there being dead silence which seemed to last for a couple of hours but was just a minute or two. The next thing she remembered was feeling this gigantic hole in the middle of her stomach, in her soul.

"Mommy and daddy are dead?" she asked as if she were in a dream and wanted to verify what was actually happening.

"Yes, darling, they are, but I love you very much, you know that, and I'm here for you, I'll take care of you precious," Aunt Catherine replied, barely being able to formulate any words herself as she was grieving over her older brother who had meant so much to her and was an inspiration to the whole family. The room began to spin and Maureen felt as if she was going to fall to one or the other side so she focused on her Aunt Catherine's face. The only color to her face was the redness of her eyes. The rest of her was as white as a ghost. Maureen fell forward into her arms and wept thinking that had she gone with them, she might be with them now. The tears fell.

The deaths of Thomas Farnsworth and Mary Farnsworth devastated the whole neighborhood and community. They had been model citizens and had raised their children with respect and with a joy for life. Billy was fourteen months younger than Maureen and didn't say much after the accident. He became very quiet and avoided the subject whenever possible. It was in the Farnsworths' last will and testament that Thomas' sister Catherine take care of the children.

It was just after the death of her parents that Matt and Maureen became the best of friends. While Maureen was out of school with the death of her parents, Matt had been out for a couple of days because his grandmother had died. "Nani" as he referred to her was his mother's mother. Her name was derived from the Czechoslovakian word "nanishka" which was slang for "grandmother." She was a vital woman even to the end. Every Sunday after church, Matt and his parents would stop by Nani's on their way home. She was always dressed up as if she had gone to church but Matt knew she never attended. It wasn't until years after her death that Matt understood the reason why she was always dressed up when they visited. She was so happy for their visit and was so excited to see her grandchild; she wanted to be seen in her finest clothes.

One Saturday, Matt's mother and father told him to get dressed, that they were going to visit Nani. Matt thought this was odd because they normally only went to visit Nani after church on Sundays. As they headed into town, Matt noticed that they weren't going in the direction of Nani's house. All of a sudden, he thought something was wrong and began to worry. He wanted to say something, but was afraid of what he might find out. They arrived at the hospital and as they got out of the car, Matt stayed inside.

"Matt, honey, how are you going to see Nani if you stay in the car?" his mother asked.

"Can't Nani come out here?" Matt questioned.

"No. She can't. You need to come with us," his mother responded.

Matt knew he couldn't sit in the car and needed to go with his mom and dad. He always obeyed them and was a good kid.

As they walked into the hospital, his eyes stared at the ground. He knew something was wrong, but he couldn't figure out what. He hated the smell of that hospital. It smelled like old socks or something used to clean wounds. While they walked down the long corridors of the hospital he looked at the people and noticed a man and a woman crying. He also noticed people with bandages on their hands, on their feet, and on their heads. It was making him sick. Just as they turned the corner, his father opened the door to his Nani's room. His mom walked in holding his hand. He could tell that his mom was very sad. Her eyes were swelling as she struggled to hold back her tears. As they approached Nani's bed, he noticed how white Nani was, how weak she looked. She didn't look like the grandmother he knew, the grandmother he'd played games with last Easter. The woman in that bed didn't look like his Nani. They spent an hour with Nani. His mom cried. His dad cried. Nani was barely able to speak and when she did, his mother had to get close to hear her. His mom picked him up and placed him on her bed. His mom helped Nani remove a pendant from her neck and she gave it to her grandchild. She then said something in Czechoslovakian that his mom translated as, "I will always love you my child, don't ever forget that. I will look out for you from the heavens above." His mom started crying, sobbing. His Nani closed her eyes and his dad helped him down from the bed.

Three days later, they were attending Nani's funeral. When he returned to school, he found out that Maureen wasn't in class because her mother and father had died. When she returned to school, he went up to her and told her that he was really sorry about the death of her mom and dad and that his grandmother had died that week, too. He told her that maybe they were all in heaven together, enjoying each other's company. He told her about his Nani and how much fun she was and how much he missed her. Likewise, she told him about her parents. She couldn't say much more because she knew she would start crying again and she didn't want to do that at school.

Matt, Maureen, and Billy roller-skated at the school on their weekends, since this was the only place they knew that didn't have a hill to conquer. Maureen recalled the time Billy had fallen, cut his knee, and was bleeding quite a bit. She tore a piece of her shirt off and placed it around his knee. She and Matt carried Billy all the way home. Each step, Maureen ensured Billy that he was going to be alright and that there was nothing to worry about. Maureen certainly showed her love and caring for her brother on that day. But caring for Maureen and Billy was getting to be too much for Catherine. Catherine phoned her older brother Russell one day to ask for his advice. As much as they did not want to split up Maureen and her brother, there was no alternative. Billy was sent to Montana to live with his Uncle Russell, who had two children of his own. Billy and Maureen would see each other whenever possible, but the distance was too far for them to see as much of each other as they wanted.

The time apart from Billy was difficult for Maureen. Her and Billy had been inseparable and played with each other all the time, no matter the game. One day they might be playing dolls, the next playing baseball in the backyard. Neither one of them had a problem with stereotypes that society placed on little boys and girls and what they should or shouldn't play. They were there for each other; that's all that mattered, until now. The first few months were terrible and contributed to Maureen's tears and depression. She got along with Aunt Catherine well enough, but it just wasn't the same. Deep down, she knew Aunt Catherine couldn't raise both her and Billy, but she resented her for not even trying. She was allowed to call Billy, but only on Saturday mornings. Their conversations were always the same—cheerful and full of laughter during the beginning of their talk, sad and tearful towards the end when either Aunt Doris or Aunt Catherine would tell them it was time to get off the phone.

There were times when Maureen thought about running away to be with Billy, but then what? She knew Uncle Russell and Aunt Doris would just send her back to Aunt Catherine.

Although Matt felt horrible for Maureen having been separated from her brother, it gave him the opportunity to enjoy playing with a sister he never had.

In addition to Matt, Maureen soon began to make more friends at school and invited them over to the house to play. Although spending time and playing with her friends after school was great and lifted her spirits, she still missed Billy whenever she sat down to dinner. She cried herself to sleep thinking how unfair life was. Why did she have to all of a sudden lose her parents and now her brother? Life wasn't fair but she knew deep down inside that she had to make the best of it. She knew one day that she and Billy would be together again but as the years passed, their connection weakened and the calls decreased. Either Maureen had an outing to go to or Billy was staying the night over at friends and wasn't going to be back until Sunday. It appeared that they were both getting on with their lives.

Matt was the only child of Michael and Stephanie Tylo, and had been raised around his father's brothers and sisters and their families. His childhood was filled with great memories of big family events as his father was one of eight children. Each year, one of them was responsible for having the entire family over for a Christmas celebration. Matt never felt like he was an only child on those occasions because the house was filled with the laughter of so many aunts and uncles and cousins. He had two cousins that were around the same age as him and often played with them. Christmas was always a time for celebration and good times spent with family. Matt loved being a part of a big family.

Matt's father worked as an engineer for one of the largest oil companies in the U.S. He often traveled throughout Europe and the Middle East. He could always tell when his father was in the Middle East because his mother, Stephanie would spend more time with him and was more sullen, obviously worried about his father. His dad was the middle son of the family and had been the only one to go to college and advance his career into the lucrative position that it was. His mom worked as a part-time nurse when the two first met but soon after marrying quit as they didn't need the money. It was more important to Matt's father that she stay at home with her son because he didn't want him raised by a stranger. Matt always looked forward to when his father returned home because he would always bring him something exotic from one of the cities he had visited. Matt had a miniature cuckoo clock from Germany and a bota from his grandfather's homeland, Spain. He also had a Buddha figurine from when his father visited Thailand.

Matt's mom always tucked him in to bed at night and would sing him a little song to "rest his mind," as she told him. Matt knew the songs weren't popular but thought that his mom created them just for him. His mom would always be the one to wake him in the morning with a cheery smile on her face and if he didn't wake, she would begin to tickle him. The morning of January 22, 1976 was different. Matt woke up to cries that sounded like they were coming from the kitchen. They were his mother's. She was talking to someone. The absence of another voice made him realize that she must be talking on the phone. As he listened, he thought that something had happened to his father but then thought that something had happened to one of his uncles. He was relieved to know that it wasn't his father but was sad to think that one of his uncles was dead, so it sounded.

Matt heard his mother coming down the hall and pretended to be asleep in his room. His mother opened the door and whispered, "Mattie, are you awake?"

She tried to hold back her tears and sniffled, "Matthew?"

Matt was too frightened to turn around and simply said, "I'm awake."

"Look at me, dear," his mother cried.

Matt swallowed the lump that was residing in his throat and turned over to look at his mother. She was pale.

"Honey, I have something to tell you and I need you to be grown up for me, okay?"

"Okay," Matt began to cry. He knew that whatever the news was, it was terrible.

"Your father was coming back home last night when the plane that he was in crashed. I got a call this morning from the government and your father's company. They are trying to find out what happened but they know there aren't any survivors." His mother moved in to hold him to her chest. "Your father is gone. He's dead."

The room darkened and Matt's heart raced. Certainly she meant to say someone else was dead, not his father. "How? Why? Are you sure?" Matt asked as he began to cry.

"I'm sure. I wouldn't tell you anything unless I was sure. If there was any doubt, believe me I would be praying now for your father to return, but it just isn't so." His mom wiped away her tears and rocked back and forth as she held him tightly.

"Do you want to come out to the kitchen with me?"

Matt could barely utter a word. His cries were now sobs. He had no control over his own breathing or voice. He managed to regain some control and said, "No. I just want to lie here for a while. I'll come out in a minute."

"Okay, honey. I love you," she said as she put him back to bed.

Matt recoiled into bed and let the flow of tears drench his sheets. All he could think about was the pain that he saw on his mother's face, how much he loved his father, and how much fun the three of them had. And now it had all ended, just like that. How could he go through life without ever seeing his father again? Who would be there to guide him, to shelter him and his mother, to comfort him when he was scared? He cried continuously for the next couple of hours until his mother came back in his room. He stopped crying and tried to show her that he was strong. Besides, he knew she was hurting even more and he didn't want to add to her pain. There was very little else that Matt remembered about that time. He had scattered memories of the funeral but remembered telling Mo when she called. She cried with him as he heard his own voice utter, "my father's dead." He wanted to believe that he was living a nightmare and that it wasn't true but when he heard himself say it, reality set in. It was true and all he had now was his mother.

Matt and Mo were as close as any brother and sister. Because they had experienced tragedy at early ages, it brought them closer together. They shared the same teacher throughout elementary school, graduated together, and when it came time to select a college for their higher education, they even attended the same university together. During their freshman year, Matt received a call from a friend with whom they had graduated and was attending the same university. He told him that one of their good friends from high school, Stuart Johnson, had been hit by a drunk driver and was dead. Stuart was a kind, gentle hearted person who never hurt anyone's feelings. He was always laughing at Matt's corny jokes and teasing Matt about being the teacher's pet in their Algebra class.

Matt disliked his Algebra teacher but for some reason she liked him and always mentioned that Matt got the highest grade on their tests. Matt couldn't stand it when she did that and would always get embarrassed. One time during class, the teacher had asked several students to come up to the chalkboard to solve a problem. Each student's attempt fell short and the problem was still unresolved. Their teacher began to lecture them on how they needed to know Algebra and how it would help them in the future and how they should feel terrible for not knowing how to solve the problem or at least get close to the solution. Stuart raised his hand and suggested that Matt attempt to solve it. Matt glared at Stuart as he sat there with a smirk on his face.

The teacher applauded Stuart for his suggestion and asked him to go up to the chalkboard and solve the problem first. She told him that if he couldn't, then she'd ask Matt. Stuart spent five minutes at the chalkboard trying to solve it. The teacher asked him to sit down and invited Matt, who contemplated on whether to solve it. He knew how to get the answer, but didn't want to solve it just to spite Stuart and the teacher. He decided he would anyway and within two minutes, the equation was solved. He and Stuart never forgot that moment and laughed about it all the time.

And now, Stuart was gone. Just like his Nani, his Uncle Paul, his Aunt Victoria, and his father. They were all gone. If it was one thing that Matt was familiar with, it was death.

CHAPTER 3

"A Year to Remember"

It was during his freshman year, spring semester that Matt realized he was gay. There had been a tennis player living in the dormitory with whom he occasionally shared glances; neither of them admitting that there was anything else going on other than a mutual liking. That was until February 4, 1979. Matt left the dorm after dinner and went for a walk around the lake. On his way, he came across Daniel, who was headed to the dorm.

"Hi, how are you?" Matt said, nervously trying to start a conversation.

"Good, what are you up to," replied Daniel.

Matt detected a little nervousness in his voice as well. This was good. "I was just going to take a walk around the lake, what about you?" Matt retorted, hoping that Daniel just might take the bait and join him.

"I was headed back to the dorm, but I don't have anything I really have to do, mind if I join you?" Daniel inquired.

"No, not at all," Matt said coolly, attempting not to appear too excited.

Matt admired Daniel and casually snuck a look at the frame of his body whenever the chance arose. All the way to the lake they had been conversing, but Matt suddenly couldn't remember a single word either one of them had said. He remembered how the sun, just before it set, highlighted Daniel's muscular legs. They talked for hours as they walked around the lake. As they stood there, admiring the moonlight as it reflected off the peaceful water, Daniel turned to Matt but didn't say a word. As Matt looked back at Daniel, their eyes felt locked to one another. Matt noticed that Daniel had the sharpest blue eyes he'd ever seen. Of course, they were probably accentuated by Daniel's tan from playing tennis, but nevertheless, they were beautiful. Nothing was said. Matt slowly felt the brush of Daniel's lips on his and then Daniel placed his arms around him and gave him the most sensual and warm hug Matt had ever felt.

Matt took a step back as if to regain his consciousness and to process what was really happening.

Just then Daniel said, "I'm sorry. I just wondered what it would be like to kiss you and I thought you wanted me to kiss you. I won't do it again if you don't want."

Matt didn't quite know what to say but as he stared at Daniel, he knew he wanted him to do it again. It felt so good, so right. He didn't say a word; he just took a step closer to Daniel and kissed him back. This kiss lasted a little longer. Matt stopped and turned away to look out at the water. His heart felt like it was beating a thousand beats per minute and felt like he needed to catch his breath.

"Is it the excitement of the moment or was it that what we are doing is wrong?" Matt thought.

Not sure what to make of the situation, Daniel confessed, "I've noticed you around for quite some time and always wanted to talk to you but I guess I was too shy. I think you are really cute. I always wondered what it would be like to kiss you or to hug you, but didn't think it would ever happen. I wasn't even sure if you were gay."

Matt responded, "I'm not sure I am gay. This is all so new to me. I mean, I like you and I've been admiring you too, I'm just not sure that this is what I want. Don't get me wrong though, it felt really nice."

Daniel was afraid where the conversation was headed so he decided to kiss Matt again. This time, he would make it a sensual kiss that would last a little longer to give Matt something to really think about. He thought Matt might stop him and turn away, but he didn't. He was as much into it as Daniel was and this pleased both of them. This time, Daniel reached around Matt's shoulders and placed his hands delicately behind his head as he kissed him. Daniel was surprised that Matt responded by placing his arms around Daniel's waste. It seemed as if the kiss lasted for hours but was probably only a minute when Matt interrupted them.

"I think I should head back to the dorm now."

Daniel knew that although Matt seemed somewhat interested in him, this was something that he needed to think about. Daniel felt comfortable that Matt would be discreet and not mention it to anyone; after all, Daniel didn't want everyone on campus to know that he was gay.

With this in mind, Daniel replied, "It is a little late, maybe we should head back."

The walk back was strange. Neither one of them spoke for the first several minutes. Daniel wanted to ask Matt if they could see each other again but knew he might appear to be too aggressive or needy. He decided not to say anything but searched for something else to say since it was so quiet.

Matt was the first to speak.

"I had a good time and I really like you Daniel. Maybe we can play tennis sometime or see a movie in town."

Daniel was taken by surprise. It was like Matt had read his mind.

"Sure, I'd like that. Let me give you my number when we get back and you can call me."

They exchanged numbers when they returned to the dorms and just before Daniel was moving in to kiss Matt again, Matt stepped back and shook his hand.

"Okay, it was good meeting you. I'll call you."

Daniel hadn't recognized someone coming up the path behind him and at first was upset that Matt was now treating him like a "study buddy." He walked away and hoped that Matt would really call him. He thought, "He really said he wasn't sure he was gay? Yeah, right. I don't know how many straight guys go around kissing other guys! Oh well, if he calls, he calls." He tried to convince himself that it really didn't matter; all the while he was hoping that Matt would call him that night. He looked forward to hearing from him but didn't want to seem too anxious.

That night, Matt debated on whether to call Daniel. He wanted to talk to him, to say something but couldn't think of anything to say. He wanted to tell him that he really did enjoy their time together but he didn't want Daniel to interpret that as he wanted to start dating him. Matt wasn't even sure how he meant it. There was just something about Daniel that he couldn't stop thinking about. Maybe it was his lips. They seemed so soft. He seemed so gentle, so caring. Maybe it was just the excitement of the situation. Maybe it was just that he was experiencing something that he had never experienced before. "Yeah, that's what it is," Matt thought. "It's just a fluke. It doesn't mean anything. So I kissed him, that doesn't mean I'm gay. It just means that, that, oh, who am I kidding?"

The conversations in Matt's head continued throughout the night. As he readied himself for bed the very thought of Daniel made his heart beat faster. He thought that if anyone saw him, they would know what he had been up to.

He would have to avoid Mo. She would know something was up and he wouldn't be able to lie to her. She would already be suspicious because it seemed like she knew where he was every minute of the day. He hadn't called her and he knew she would be suspicious. "I'll just tell her I went to the lake to think about life and when I got back I was really tired and went straight to bed," he thought.

As he lay in bed, he knew he needed to think about what had happened. To think about how he felt. To think about what it all meant.

Although he didn't know what to think about Daniel, he did know that it was different than when he was with a girl. He thought back to Laura Stevens and his freshman year in high school. He and Laura frequently went to the movies and would make out occasionally, but they were more friends than they were boyfriend and girlfriend. Matt had plenty of excuses why they shouldn't have sex. There was the "wait until marriage" excuse, the "I don't think I'm ready for that yet" excuse, and the "I think we should take it slow" excuse. The thought of sex scared him. It just didn't seem right. He didn't know why he felt that way it was just a matter of fact. He thought that maybe she wasn't the one and that he just had to wait until he met the perfect someone who would make him feel so comfortable that sex wouldn't be scary. Little did he know that it would be another boy who would make him feel that.

When he and Laura made out, it seemed rehearsed as if he were acting out the emotions, playing a part in a play. There was a disconnect between his actions and his feelings.

And now it seemed different. He felt so comfortable with Daniel. These were real, pure emotions. Still, he couldn't help but think that the feelings he was sharing were wrong.

It was around four o'clock in the morning that Matt finally fell asleep. When he awoke at eight o'clock in the morning, he was extremely tired, but very excited. He woke up thinking about Daniel and wondered if Daniel was thinking about him as well. Although he wanted to call him and wish him a good morning, he knew he was going to be late for his nine o'clock class if he didn't get ready at that moment.

His classes ended at three o'clock in the afternoon and he headed back to the dorm. He ran into Mo on the way.

"Hey stranger, what have you been up to? I haven't spoken to you in at least twenty-four hours!" probed Mo.

"I've been doing something called attending classes. It's something you do when you are in college. Ever heard of it?" Matt responded.

"Well, someone's in a fine mood today. What the hell's wrong with you?" Mo replied.

"I'm just tired that's all. I was up late studying and I only got four hours of sleep. I'm going back to the dorm now to take a nap, what are you doing?"

"I'm headed to my last class. Want to catch dinner together? I'll come by your room after my class, okay?" Mo asked.

"Okay, that sounds fine. Sorry about my smart ass comment before," Matt said, realizing how snotty he must have sounded.

"That's alright. I'm used to it," Mo said with a smile on her face.

Matt went back to his room and picked up the phone. He hung up the phone. He picked up the phone. He hung up the phone and picked it up again. He placed the call. Daniel's roommate answered the phone. Matt wasn't sure what to say but just told his roommate to tell Daniel that he called. Matt decided to take advantage of some quiet time and take that much needed nap.

At five o'clock in the afternoon, the phone rang. Matt, jumped to answer it but he was only half awake and thought it was probably Mo calling as she returned from class.

"Hello," Matt said in a groggy voice.

"Hi Matt. It's Daniel," he heard on the other end of the line.

"Oh, hi. How are you?" Matt answered trying to regain his thoughts.

"I'm fine. My roommate said you called," Daniel responded.

"Yeah, I was just calling to say Hi and find out how you were." Matt knew this sounded corny, but didn't know what else to say. He was still fighting the drowsiness he was feeling from being asleep. "I had to call you and hear your voice. I thought about you a lot last night and wanted to call but didn't," Matt confessed.

"What were you thinking about," Daniel said coolly.

"Just about what happened and how nice it was," Matt replied.

"I enjoyed it too. So, when can I see you again?" Daniel inquired.

"I'm not sure. I'm heading to dinner with a friend in a little bit and I have to study for a midterm tonight but I might be able to be persuaded to take a break," Matt said.

"Okay, how about I call you later tonight and see how your studying is going. Maybe we can go on a walk to the lake again," Daniel suggested.

"That sounds nice. I'll talk to you later. Bye."

"Bye for now," Daniel said.

Matt hung up the phone and felt excited although he wondered what he was doing. He knew he really wanted to see Daniel—whether seeing him was right or wrong—that was all he knew and that's what he was going to do.

Matt was surprised that Mo didn't interrogate him at dinner about where he had been the night before or why he was really so tired. That made him feel better, knowing he didn't have to lie to her. He hated the idea of lying to Mo, his very best friend. After dinner, he headed back to the dorm where he began to study for his midterm. Around nine-thirty in the evening, the phone rang. It was Daniel asking him when he wanted to head to the lake. Although Matt wanted to study a bit more, he said he was available then. Daniel agreed and they met halfway between their dorms and headed to the lake.

On their walk, they talked about classes, friends, everything but how each of them was feeling. When they reached a remote part of the lake where Daniel knew they would have some privacy, he pointed out that the sky was so clear, every last star could be seen. He lay down on the grass and asked Matt to join him. Matt lay down next to Daniel and they stared up at the stars. It was so quiet. Matt's view of the stars was all of a sudden blocked by Daniels' face. He was moving in for a kiss. Matt waited for the moment to happen and was glad that Daniel was making the first move. As they kissed, Daniel moved closer to Matt. They hugged and kissed and stared at the stars for what must have been an hour until they heard people coming. They jumped up in a hurry and began walking down the path back to the dorms.

Daniel turned to Matt and asked, "Can I see your dorm room? I'm so jealous that you get to have a room all to yourself."

Matt wasn't sure if this was such a good idea but was enticed by the thought and said, "Sure, why not? I just can't stay up too late tonight. I have to get some sleep!"

They were no sooner in the door when Daniel began kissing Matt. Matt stopped him to lock the door to his room and before he knew it, Daniel was leading him towards Matt's bed. As Matt fell on the bed, Daniel lay on top of him and began kissing him. All of a sudden it seemed like Daniel was an octopus with eight arms and hands that were making their way all over Matt. He moved his hand down Matt's torso and began to rub his crotch. Matt could barely catch his breath but managed to utter, "I think you should stop it." Either Daniel didn't hear Matt or he didn't want to listen. Matt repeated himself, "I think you should stop Daniel!"

Daniel responded, "Why? I thought you were fine with this?"

"I thought I was, too. I mean, I am, I think I am but not now. I'm not ready for this. This is happening too fast. I thought you wanted to see my dorm room," Matt responded.

"Get real. Did you really think I wanted to come back to your dorm room to see it? To see how you decorated it?" Daniel replied.

"Well, no, but I thought we could at least talk or…. I don't know," Matt said at a loss for words.

"I'm not sure you are ready for this Matt. Why don't you think about it a little bit more and call me when you're ready," Daniel snapped.

"Give me a break, Daniel, I'm not as comfortable with all of this as you are," Matt replied.

"I know. I just thought that…never mind. I should go," Daniel said frustratingly.

"I'm sorry," Matt muttered as Daniel closed the door.

It was difficult for Matt to call Daniel now. He realized that Daniel didn't know him at all and only wanted to fool around. Although he was interested in that, it was happening way too fast for Matt. There were things that he knew. He knew that he liked Daniel, physically. He knew Daniel was funny and that he liked his personality. He knew that he wanted to see him again, to kiss him again. He also knew that Daniel wasn't a very patient boy. There were also things he didn't know. He didn't know how Daniel was able to accept that he was gay so easily. He didn't know how Daniel would react if they were to get together again. He didn't know how he felt and whether being gay was something that he wanted.

Three days went by before Matt finally called Daniel. When he did, his roommate answered the phone and Matt left a message for Daniel to call him back. Another three days went by and Matt hadn't heard back from Daniel. On Friday night just before *Dallas* was about to air on the small, thirteen inch, color television screen that Matt had in his room, the phone rang. It was Daniel. When Matt asked him what took him so long to return his call he said that he had tried but wasn't able to get a hold of Matt. Matt thought that this was probably a lie but decided to give Daniel the benefit of the doubt. Why hadn't he tried calling him later in the evening like he had done before? He then realized that it didn't matter since he was talking to him now. Daniel asked Matt what he had been up to and apologized for coming on so strong the last time they were together.

"I'm not sure what came over me. I guess I was just a little horny or something," Daniel said.

"That's alright," Matt responded, "I would like to see you again, but I really just want to be friends."

Matt couldn't believe what he was saying. This wasn't anything that he had rehearsed so where was it coming from? Matt knew he didn't want to be friends, but it must have been the pressure that Daniel put on him that made him react this way.

"Friends?" Daniel replied. "I thought we could be a little more than just friends."

Matt thought about what he wanted to say, what he should say, and then told him, "Well, "more than friends" might work, but you have to give me some time. This is all new to me and I don't want to rush into anything."

"So what you are saying is that you want a casual relationship," Daniel retorted.

"I guess," Matt responded, thinking about what a "casual relationship" really meant.

The conversation continued as they talked about their classes and what they were planning on doing over the coming weekend. They tentatively made plans to see a movie at the school theatre on Saturday night. Matt would have to make up a lie to tell Maureen why he wouldn't be meeting up with her. Matt quickly ended the conversation as *Dallas* had already started and he hated missing anything from his favorite soap opera.

CHAPTER 4

"Acceptance"

Matt and Daniel never met that Saturday night and they never got together again. They occasionally saw each other at the dining commons or around campus, but the conversation was always superficial and didn't lead to anything more. Matt figured Daniel found someone else to pine after and possibly got what he wanted. This wasn't too upsetting to Matt as he figured he had a lot to think about and didn't want to start something he knew he couldn't finish.

He spent the next three years admiring other boys and wishing he knew why he was marveling at them, why he fantasized about them kissing him, and why they appeared naked in his dreams, lying next to him. "When is this going to end," he would ask himself. He even tried dating girls in school, but he wasn't into it and didn't feel comfortable making out with a girl. So, he decided to spend his time with his friends and to enjoy their company. Maybe if he just forgot about it all together and stopped analyzing what he felt, everything would fall into place and he would find his direction.

Six months prior to graduating, Matt got a job at one of the largest financial institutions in downtown San Francisco. He went through five interviews and thought that he would never get the job. The position combined his interests in the investment world and information technology. He would be a part of a team that was responsible for analyzing the data flow of international securities held by the company's different funds and recommending improvements with the process. When he got the call telling him that they were offering him the position he was ecstatic but played it cool. He said he would think about it after he got the offer letter and benefits package they said they would be express mailing to him overnight. He knew he would accept the position but didn't want to seem too anxious.

The last six months of school were the best six months of his time at the university. While others were worrying about finding a job, he was free to concentrate on his studies and have fun before entering the corporate world.

He joined his new firm on July 1, 1983, and was surprised to find that most of the people he met were very nice and down to earth. He had imagined that his co-workers would be very driven and competitive like his classmates, but he found them to be just the opposite. They were very willing to help him learn the ropes of the firm and how it operated. He soon became friends with many of them. One of them, Cassie Montgomery, started with the firm the week before Matt started, so there was a natural bond with them from the beginning. They became friends almost immediately. Her personality was very similar to Mo's although she didn't look anything like her. Cassie was funny but could be serious at the same time. She was always willing to help out a friend or a co-worker or listen to them talk through their problems. She was a brunette with shoulder length hair and had a smile that made you feel comfortable as soon as you saw it. Her eyes were brown but not a dark brown. They had specks of gold in them that one normally sees with hazel eyes. At first, Matt thought they were contacts, but then one day she wore glasses and he knew they had to be real. She had the most beautiful, smooth skin. It was no surprise that she had plenty of dates with men she met while out with her girlfriends. She was always the first to begin talking to strangers and to make friends right off the bat. She was anything but shy, unlike her friends. When she went out her goal was "to have fun, not to necessarily meet someone" as she always said. It seemed to work for her, much to the jealousy of her friends.

Matt often put in long hours at the firm, trying to make a good impression and it worked. His supervisor and team leads adored him. He was efficient, creative, and timely. When assigned a project, his supervisors and co-workers who were dependent on his project, were always confident that he would complete it within the timeframe given. Occasionally, he and Cassie went out to dinner when they worked late. Cassie didn't work late much nor did she appear to be as happy with her job as was Matt. One night, Matt invited Mo to join them because he knew that she was working late on a proposal for a new advertisement. At dinner, Cassie observed how well Matt and Mo got along and asked, "Why aren't you two dating?"

Matt and Mo started laughing but for different reasons. Matt was the first to respond.

"I think of her as a sister, I don't think I could date my own sister! Besides, we are such great friends; I would hate to ruin that."

Mo said, "I don't think I've ever thought of Matt in that regard. Maybe it's like Matt said, we think of each other as siblings. It would be too weird. Besides, he's too picky."

The conversation went back and forth between Matt and Mo as they argued who was the pickier. Cassie finally had to break up the debate and declare neither one of them the winner.

Later that night, Matt thought about what Cassie had said. Why wasn't he attracted to Mo? Why wasn't he attracted to Cassie? They were both very pretty women and were a lot of fun to be around. Why he was asking himself that question was a waste of time. He knew why he wasn't attracted to them. He was attracted to men.

One night, he decided to go out by himself and he would head out to the Castro, the gay district of San Francisco. As much as he was curious, he was excited and nervous. So nervous in fact that he felt ill to his stomach but he knew he needed to get out. He left right after work around seven o'clock and took the streetcar there. It was convenient because the streetcar went down Market and turned around at the heart of the gay area. As he took his seat on the streetcar, he wondered what he was doing, what he was expecting, where he would go. It didn't matter to him, he just wanted to go out and see what it was like.

There were a couple of guys on the train who were obviously gay and he thought, "They are so blatantly gay. I'm not like that. I'm nothing like that. What am I doing?" As he contemplated getting off the streetcar and heading home, he thought about his alternative. He would go home, make dinner and sit in front of the TV or go for a run as he liked to do. No. He was going to go there and look around. If he didn't like it, he could always head home after that. After all, it wasn't far from his home in Diamond Heights.

When the train stopped at Market and 17th streets, he got off. It was crowded on the streets. He saw all kinds of people. Certainly they weren't all gay, were they? As he walked around the streets, taking in the scene, the people, and the bars, he noticed one in particular that seemed like it was attracting the kind of guys that he always found good-looking. He walked past it several times trying to take that step inside but couldn't. He was scared. This was a whole new world; one that he didn't have a clue about. How should he act?

What would he say if someone started talking to him? His head was spinning and his heart was pounding. After thinking about how stupid he must look walking back and forth down the street, he finally worked up the courage to go inside. It was a dark and crowded bar. He stepped up to the bar and ordered a rum and coke and took it towards the end of the bar where he stood and admired everyone. They were so cute. They didn't fit the mold that he had in his head of someone who was gay and certainly didn't remind him of the flamboyant gay men on the streetcar he'd seen earlier. In fact, if anyone saw these guys outside of this bar, he was sure they wouldn't be able to tell that they were gay. He thought about how he had debated on whether to go out and how nervous he was and how ridiculous it was. As he stood at the end of the bar, he watched how they interacted. He was sure they all knew that this was his first time here. He felt uncomfortable and knew it showed. He felt a little awkward since he was there by himself with no one to talk to. He decided to have another drink. As he stood there, he listened to the music and thought about how this music was so much better than that played in the straight bars he had been to with Mo and Cassie. He noticed that his drink was gone and decided to have another. Although he was still somewhat nervous, he was surprised at how much more comfortable he was getting. That was, until James came over and introduced himself. He was extremely cute. He was six feet tall, sandy blonde hair with blue eyes. He was wearing a polo shirt and khaki pants. He was very fit and had a swimmer's body.

"You look like you're enjoying yourself. Like he music?" he said.

"Uh, yeah," Matt stammered.

"Hi, my name's James, what's yours?" he said.

"Matt," was all he could say after it took him a while to think of his name.

"I haven't seen you around here before, are you visiting?" James asked.

"No, I moved here about six months ago and am just now hitting the scene," Matt said, trying desperately not to sound too nerdy or as if it was the first time he had gone out.

"Well, how do you like the place?" James said.

"Oh, I like it a lot. Do you come here often?" Matt said.

"Yeah. It's one of my favorites, but if you want to dance, the Dive is nice," James replied, "Do you like to dance?"

Matt responded, "Yes. I love to dance, especially if they're playing good music."

"Good. How would you like to head there a little later?" James asked.

"Sure." Matt was excited about the opportunity and wanted to dance, especially with James since he was so cute. Matt remembered Daniel and couldn't help feel that James was a bit of a player as well. He seemed so smooth in his delivery. "I bet he does this all the time. I bet he finds a new guy every week," Matt thought before shutting his inner voice up.

An hour later and two drinks later, Matt and James left the bar. On their way to the Dive, James suggested that he stop by his apartment to change as he was wearing a turtleneck and wanted to wear something less warm. James lived a couple of blocks away from the bar so the trip to James' apartment would be just a short detour from their destination. Matt was feeling somewhat lightheaded because he hadn't been drinking in quite a while and on Friday nights he was usually a little more tired than other nights because of the long hours he worked during the week. As they entered James' apartment, James noticed that his roommates weren't home and asked Matt if he wanted to wait in the living room or if he wanted to wait in his bedroom while he changed.

Although Matt was feeling drunk, he decided to wait in the living room because he wasn't sure what might happen if he went into the bedroom. He had known James for only four hours and wasn't sure what he had in mind. While Matt waited he looked around the living area and thought it was odd that there weren't any pictures anywhere. How many people didn't have pictures of friends, families, even pets they liked to display?

"Oh well," he thought, "maybe he doesn't have a camera."

The living room was tucked away in the back part of the old Victorian house that had been turned into three separate units. Although the apartment was very old, it had a lot of character. The ceiling was decorated with crown molding and antique light fixtures. Around the light fixtures were elaborately designed patterns that accentuated the light fixture perfectly. It's too bad that the paint on the walls was a bland white. Matt thought about how beautiful the room could be if it was painted in another color, any color. A nice avocado color or a coffee color would look very nice with white trim, he thought as he entertained himself.

James came out after only a couple of minutes and referring to his black short-sleeved and somewhat see-through button shirt said, "So what do you think? I think I'll be more comfortable now, what about you?"

"That looks nice, what's it made of," Matt said as he stood up to feel the fabric.

As Matt stood up he felt a little light-headed and fell a little closer towards James than he had planned. James immediately grabbed Matt by the waist and kissed him.

"Why don't you sit down for a bit before we head out?" James instructed, "I'll get you some water. How's that sound?"

"That would be nice. Thank you," Matt replied, sitting down on the sofa.

"Here you go." James approached him.

Matt took a sip of water and turned to his right to place the glass down on the end table. As he did, he felt James sit down beside him on the sofa. When he turned back to ask James how long he had lived there, James placed his hands on each side of Matt's head and kissed him. Matt returned the kiss and couldn't believe how much different kissing James was than any other kiss he'd experienced. James' lips were so soft and supple. Matt was kissing him back and soon his hands were busy stroking James' hair and pushing his head towards his to feel the kiss and the heat that was building between them. Matt's head was spinning. He didn't know whether it was the alcohol or the passion that was making him feel this way so he continued to take breaks in between their kissing to drink his water.

As James continued kissing Matt, he began unbuttoning his shirt and began kissing him on the neck. This excited Matt even more and soon his hands moved from caressing his hair to his waist. Matt was pulling James closer and closer to him as they fell sideways to cover the length of the couch. James moved from Matt's neck to around the side of his face and found his ear that he started to lick.

Matt thought he was in heaven. This felt so good. James' warm breath on his ear and the licking was driving Matt crazy. There was no time to think about whether this was right or wrong. He knew it was right. Their passion felt so incredibly right, so natural; there was no way he was stopping. Although a small part of his brain was concerned about where this was headed, he wasn't listening to it. Matt began to nuzzle James' neck and kiss him passionately. He could tell this made James even more excited.

"Damn, you are a good kisser," James said, out of breath.

Matt sat up for a minute. "You're not too bad yourself."

He felt very proud of himself because he had never been complimented like this before. The only thing Matt could think about was that he didn't want this to end. He wanted to absorb every minute and appreciate what was happening. For the first time in his life, Matt truly felt alive and a connection with another guy that he had yearned for for so long. Matt was getting very excited and could see that James was, too. As James moved back to kissing Matt on the lips he slowly stood up and grabbed Matt by the hand, standing him upright.

"Let's go into my bedroom, just in case my roommates come home," James said.

Matt didn't say anything but instead followed James to his bedroom. All the way towards his bedroom, James was kissing and fondling Matt. They stopped periodically to gently kiss each other's necks. Matt's hands were busy feeling James' torso. He didn't seem to have an ounce of fat on him. As they entered the tiny bedroom, James gently pushed Matt onto the bed and laid on top of him. He began unbuttoning Matt's shirt as Matt reciprocated, not sure what he should be doing, but he was going with his instincts. James was having difficulties with one of the buttons while Matt had completed his task. James finished with the last button and took of Matt's shirt before taking off his own. He returned to laying on top of Matt and moving away from his lips, James made his way down Matt's neck to his nipples.

He began kissing them and massaging them with his tongue. This was the first time that Matt had ever experienced anything like this and thought he would explode. How could something like this feel so good? He wondered. As James moved from one nipple to the other, Matt massaged James's head. As James moved back to Matt's face, he stopped along the way to kiss and nibble at his neck and then back to the ear. "Oh, the ear, not the ear," Matt thought as he could feel a small wet spot in the crouch of his pants. James made it back to Matt's lips where the kisses were even more passionate and stronger than before. Matt decided to reciprocate and holding James by the waist turned him onto the bed. Matt was now on top of James and began to move from his lips to his neck to his nipples.

This had an immediate effect on James as he started to moan. Matt thought he needed to do something else so it wouldn't appear that he was just "following along" and repeating exactly what James had done, so he began to lick the center of his stomach and down to wear James' pants began. Just when he got to James' belly button, he heard the front door of the apartment open.

"Anyone home," bellowed one of James' roommates.

"Ah, shit!" James whispered. He didn't say a word and waited to hear what his roommate was going to do. He heard the water faucet and steps toward the other bedroom.

"I think he's going to bed," James continued, "Now where were we?"

James looked back at Matt and saw that he was passed out. He tried to arouse him but Matt wasn't budging. When Matt awoke he noticed it was three-thirty in the morning and his head was pounding. As he lay there, he wondered what he was supposed to do. Should he stay until morning? Was James expecting him to stay? He felt extremely awkward because he knew he had passed out and was sure James didn't get what he had hoped for. Maybe he should just sneak out. After all, the affects of the alcohol had worn off and he knew he wasn't about to do anything else. Although he had had fun, he was holding out for someone who was special, someone with whom he felt a deep connection. James wasn't him.

He decided to say that he was going to go home and then judge James' reaction as to whether he should stay or not. He moved again but James didn't awaken. Matt nudged him and James stirred. "Hey," James mumbled, still half asleep.

"I think I'm going to head home now. I didn't realize it was so late," Matt said, waiting for James' reaction.

"Okay. Thanks for tonight. It was great," replied James.

Matt wasn't sure how to interpret what James said but didn't worry about it. What he wanted to do was to go home where he could be comfortable. Matt got dressed and looked back at James who was lying on the bed, naked.

"Alright, well I guess I'm going to catch a taxi," Matt said struggling with what he should say and what he should do. Just as Matt was heading out of James' door, he heard James.

"Wait."

Matt was sure that James had awakened from his current state of sleepiness and was going to ask him to stay.

"Let me walk you out," James continued.

As Matt reached the bottom of the stairs, he looked back. James was already gone, probably back to bed, Matt thought.

Matt walked the two blocks necessary to catch a taxi. His shame of passing out quickly turned to elation as he recounted what had happened. Even if James was a player, the experience was good and he didn't regret it.

Matt went home and slept until noon on Saturday. When he woke, he thought about what had happened and thought for a minute it had been a dream but it hadn't been. He felt bad. He thought about how degrading it was to have picked up someone in a bar and gone home with him. Although he enjoyed the experience, he felt sleazy, and headed for the bathroom where he took a long, hot shower.

He struggled with his feelings for several weeks, dying to tell someone, anyone, but who could he tell? He was afraid to tell Mo because she might be turned off by it and judge him or worse, avoid him because she might be uncomfortable with the whole idea of him sleeping with another man that he barely knew. Cassie wasn't that good of a friend yet to discuss something so personal. He was friends with several people at work and there was this one guy, Eric, who Matt thought was gay. Eric worked in another business unit but on the same floor as Matt. Eric was part of a group that was responsible for making sure that the company obtained the most timely and accurate prices for their securities as possible. Eric was starting his fifth year with the company. Matt's first project was to map out the data flow and he had worked with Eric to cover his part of the process. They had talked a lot about the company, their co-workers and how much they enjoyed their jobs. In a short time frame, they had become friends and often met for lunch or went out with others from work for happy hour.

Matt entertained the idea of telling Eric that he was gay. He decided to ask Eric if he wanted to go to lunch one day and test the waters. He and Eric got along well, but Matt wasn't attracted to Eric. Eric had brown hair that was pulled back into a pony tail. He stood around five feet eight and was somewhat husky. Eric was extremely nice and Matt found that they were able to carry on a conversation for hours without searching for words. Most of their conversations were centered on work and rarely delved into their personal lives.

Towards the end of their lunch, Eric turned to Matt and asked, "So what do you do for fun Matt? I mean, do you go out a lot? To bars, to clubs, what? We've known each other for almost six months and I don't think we've ever discussed anything outside of work."

"I don't really go out much. I don't know too many people in the city yet, so I'm not sure where to go. When I do go out it's with one of my friends, Maureen, and we usually go to one of the clubs down on Eleventh Street. Where do you usually go?" Matt queried.

"Well, I usually head to one of the bars or clubs in the Castro." Eric was really saying, "I'm gay in case you hadn't figured it out."

"I thought so," Matt acknowledged.

"What?" Eric was looking at Matt with a puzzled look on his face.

"Oh, nothing. I meant that I figured there were cool bars down there." Matt tried to save himself from what was an awkward moment.

"If you've never been to the Castro, maybe sometime we can go after work. You know, for dinner and maybe step into a bar. Don't get me wrong, not like a date or anything, I just thought you might want to see what it's like. It's not really as scary as people make it seem and there aren't a lot of people trying to hit on you. Besides, if we're together you can always tell anyone who tries to hit on you that you are with me. I think it's fun to take my straight friends there. They always have so much fun because many of the places play such good music and everyone is usually very nice and happy, or should I say 'gay.'" Eric chuckled.

"Sure. That would be fun," Matt said laughingly.

He later thought about it and began to worry. What would happen if they went to the same bar where he had met James and what if James approached him and sold him out? What would he say to Eric then? He would just have to steer away from that bar and the Dive since he knew James frequented those places.

He wanted to tell Eric that he was gay too, but couldn't find the words. After years of thinking he could change, that he could force himself to like women and date them, Matt knew it was impossible. He spent countless nights crying himself to sleep, praying that he could change-Praying that he could be straight and asking himself and God why he had to feel the things he felt.

From the first time he met Daniel in college until now, he couldn't stop thinking about boys. If there was a girl and a guy standing next to each other, his eyes would always focus on the guy and admire him. He would scan him from his shoes to the top of his head. He felt something inside—an emotion. It was something he wasn't sure of, but there was something there, buried deep inside, hidden from anyone for years, including himself. A very strong emotion that almost seemed to be screaming at him, telling him to follow his heart and he would be fine. "But society thinks this is so wrong, how can it be right? How can this be me?" Matt often wondered.

It was a warm fuzzy feeling and he would think back to the kiss that he and Daniel had shared. He would fantasize about feeling Daniel against him, naked. The very thought of it made him smile. How could he dismiss those feelings? How could he deal with them? For years, Matt thought about suicide. He didn't want to be gay. He hated the thought of coming out and being subjected to people pointing at him, ridiculing him, calling him names, treating him as if he were a second class citizen. How could he live this way? How would he ever be able to tell anyone what he was feeling? There were nights where he would pray that he would die. He didn't care about anyone else; he just wanted the yearning for men to go away. He wanted the pain to go away. He wanted to be normal. The tears would flow down his cheeks until he fell asleep.

He felt the struggle going on inside him and wanted it to stop. Part of him wanted to know what it was like to be with another man, and the other part of him was telling him to shut up and forget about it. He told himself that he was being selfish and that he should get over the feelings he had for other men. He wasn't raised to be gay. He could only think about how disappointed his mother and father would be. What a failure he was. Dying would be so much easier than facing all that.

The turmoil had taken its toll. Matt was frequently ill. Every year he would come down with the flu and later get an infection of some kind that his doctor couldn't explain. He'd get a prescription for antibiotics which would cure him until the next illness. He thought, "I am twenty-three-years-old and I can't live like this anymore." It was 1984 and Matt had suffered enough. He had been dealing with this battle for nearly ten years and it had to stop.

A week had passed since he and Eric had lunch and Matt decided to call him. He told Eric that he needed to talk to him and Eric suggested they meet for lunch.

"No, that won't do. I need to talk to you about something personal. Can we meet after work sometime this week?" Matt inquired.

"Sure Matt. What's wrong? You sound so different. Is everything okay?" Eric said with genuine concern in his voice.

"Yeah, something's just been bugging me and I need to talk to someone about it," Matt said.

"Well, by all means, let's meet after work tonight. If you want, you can come over to my place and I can cook us something. My roommate has a class on Wednesday nights so he won't be home," Eric suggested.

"Okay, that would be great. Thanks Eric. I'll come by your cubicle around six o'clock. Does that work?" asked Matt.

"That's fine," Eric replied.

When they got to Eric's, Eric opened a bottle of red wine and they sat on in the living room. Matt was sitting on a lazy boy chair that was pushed up against one of the corners of the small living room and Eric sat on the sofa, next to Matt's chair. Matt had rehearsed his speech several times in which he would tell Eric that he was gay but for some reason, he couldn't remember anything now and was feeling somewhat faint and he struggled for the words.

"Eric, how did you get so comfortable with the fact that you are gay?" Matt asked.

Eric was surprised with the question and concerned about the direction of the conversation, "Uh…I…uh…Well, I struggled with it for several years and then I realized that it was who I was and that I was fighting something that was part of my being, why?"

"Because, I think I'm gay. I mean, I am gay. I wish I weren't, but I am. I know that and I can't stand it. You seem so comfortable with it and I don't know if I can ever get to the point where I don't feel miserable about it." Matt began to cry. "I've wished and prayed that my feelings would go away and they haven't. I can't deal with it anymore and the worst part is that I have no one I can turn to. I don't know what to do. I feel like I'm all alone for the first time in my life. Like I'm drifting out to sea and my whole life is changing and I don't even know who I am," he said.

Eric moved closer to Matt and put his hand on his knee.

"This isn't easy. It never is. I went through the same thing before I accepted the fact that I'm gay. That's why it's so easy for me now. I refuse to feel like shit because I'm gay. There's nothing wrong with me and there's nothing wrong with you. That's what you need to focus on. I know what you are feeling. We all know what you are feeling and have all been there before. You can't forget that either. You are NOT alone! Not at all. Not by any means," Eric sympathized.

"If I'm not alone, why do I feel so miserable? Why do I feel like I just want to shrivel up and die? Why me?" Matt lamented.

Eric continued with his advice.

"Matt, you can't blame yourself for how you feel. We feel things because we are human beings. It is how God made us. There are people who think we have a choice. That we decide we want to be gay. I don't think I'll ever understand their point of view. Why would anyone 'choose' to be gay? Why would they 'choose' to be subject to name calling like 'queer,' 'faggot,' 'sissy,' 'pansy,' and all the others? Why would someone 'choose' not to be able to have a child of their own? Why would we 'choose' to be ridiculed and made fun of? Why would we 'choose' to be minorities? Why would we 'choose' a life that was harder than others? We wouldn't! We don't! It is something that is within us. It is something that is deep down in our flesh and bones. To deny what you are feeling doesn't do anyone any good. People love you Matt. I'm sure your parents and friends do. I know everyone at work loves you. They are always talking about how great you are and how funny you are and how you make them laugh. Do you think all that's going to stop because they know you are gay? You probably do, because I thought that too. You know what? It isn't true. They will still love you. Being gay isn't what you are, it's an aside. You ARE Matt Tylo. You are a good looking, intelligent, funny, hard-working, and caring individual who happens to be gay. That's how you need to look at your life."

Matt stopped crying and thought about Eric's advice.

"Can you record that so I can listen to it over and over again?" Matt said, trying to lighten up the conversation a bit.

"Listen, Matt. For you to come this far with your emotions, to be able to turn to me and tell me this, well, it is one of the biggest steps you'll ever take. It's your first step to acceptance. We all need someone with whom we can trust and confide in. I'm glad you turned to me," Eric said.

"I am too. I feel much better but I still don't know what to do next. I guess I really am gay, aren't I?" Matt said trying to get accustomed to the fact that he was, indeed, gay.

"So does this mean that you really do want to go out the bars with me?" laughed Eric.

"Well, to be honest, I've already been out at one of the bars," confided Matt.

"Really? Do tell, Matt. How was it? What happened?" Eric asked.

Matt went on to tell Eric the story of his encounter with James and how it made him feel. They spent the whole evening talking about Eric's experience and how he dealt with "coming out" to his parents, friends, and some of his co-workers. It was one of the best conversations Matt ever had. They talked until one o'clock in the morning when Matt realized it was so late and apologized for keeping Eric up so late. Eric didn't mind as he expressed to Matt, "One of the best things about our gay community is that there is always someone you can turn to and confide in. We have our own little family within the community. Don't ever forget that. And when the time arises, you will be there when someone needs to confide in you."

CHAPTER 5

"Rollercoaster Ride"

Matt finally accepted that he was gay and started hanging out with Eric. Each night he went out with him, he had to create an excuse for Mo because he still hadn't told her the truth. Still, it felt as if he was living dual lives. On one hand, he was able to be his true self while he was out with Eric because Eric was showing him the gay life. On the other hand, he was able to be his old self when he went out with Mo. He hated the fact that he couldn't share his other life with her, but he didn't know how she would react. He couldn't tell her just yet. When they did get together, they would meet for dinner and then go dancing at one of the straight clubs. Mo liked to dance so Matt didn't feel too awkward when they were out since he liked to dance as well.

It was December, 1984 and Matt was attending his first firm holiday party. He asked Maureen to go with him. She obliged and bought the most elegant cocktail dress. It was a black, crushed velvet dress with thin shoulder straps that highlighted her soft shoulders. There were no frills about the form fitting dress; however it was how she accentuated it that made it so beautiful. Mo was wearing a diamond necklace that her mother used to wear when she attended formal gatherings. It sparkled and matched her bracelet. She had her hair worn up with little curly strands that fell down the sides of her face. She looked like one of the models off of *Vanity Fair*. Matt was dressed in a traditional tuxedo that complimented Mo's dress ever so nicely.

When they arrived, Matt saw Eric who was there alone. They went up to him and Matt introduced him to Mo. They sat at the same table and talked about everything and everyone. They had several drinks and had a wonderful dinner. The three of them even went on the dance floor together and danced practically every dance. It was around midnight that the party started to fizzle out and people started leaving. Eric asked Matt and Mo if they were headed anywhere else or if they were just going to go home. Mo said she was somewhat tired from the long week and wanted to go home. Matt thought about taking Mo home and then meeting up with Eric later that night but couldn't find an opportune time to discuss it with him. Instead, he said he was going to take Mo home and then he was going home himself. Matt thought about it and didn't really want to go out to the Castro district dressed in his tuxedo and knew that by the time he got home, he would rather go to bed than to change his clothes and go out again. That was a weakness of his and he knew it. If he went home after work, he'd get too comfortable and decide to stay in rather than go out and meet people. He hated to go out by himself because it made him feel lonelier. Wherever he went, it seemed like everyone else was out with their friends and it was difficult to approach them. At least at home he didn't have to worry about making small conversation with someone he hardly knew. Even though he was more comfortable staying at home, he struggled with what he knew he should do. He should go out and meet someone. He wasn't going to meet anyone in his apartment. Matt just knew he would die a bitter and lonely old man.

On the way back to Mo's, she mentioned that Eric seemed to be a lot of fun and that she was glad that Matt had made a friend.

"He must be fun to hang out with. I didn't realize you guys did so much together. How come you never invite me when you guys go out?" she asked.

"He is fun. We have a lot in common. It's funny, but we never are at a loss of words together. It seems like we can just talk and talk and talk. Kind of like you and me," Matt answered, avoiding the discussion as to why he didn't invite Mo out when they partied together.

They were now in front of Mo's apartment when she said, "I think he's gay."

"What? Really?" Matt searched for words but didn't know how to react.

"Come on, you should know as much as you hang out together," She said.

"Well, yeah, he is," he replied.

"I knew it. I'm always so intuitive you know. I haven't lost my touch," she proclaimed.

"That's why we have so much in common," Matt said.

"What?"

Matt's heart was beating faster and faster, "that's why we have so much in common." He couldn't believe he had just said that. What was he thinking?

"I heard you the first time but what do you mean, Matt? What are you telling me?" she urged.

With his heart now beating faster and his face completely flushed, he replied, "I'm trying to tell you that I'm gay, too."

Mo sat there, staring at Matt. Matt was terrified. How was she going to react? What was taking so long? It seemed like everything was moving in slow motion. He thought he was going to pass out. What had happened to the air? How come he wasn't getting any? Just when he felt the color drop from his face, Mo said, "You're gay?"

"Yes."

"How long has this been going on?"

"Well, I've known for several years, but I'm finally accepting it now."

"I thought so." Mo stood there with a half smile on her face as if she had just solved the case of the missing corpse.

"What? You thought so? How come you never said anything?" Matt questioned.

"Why didn't you? Matt, I think I've always known but I wasn't about to ask you. We've been friends for so long. You've never had a girlfriend. I've noticed how you look at other men. I think I first thought about it back in college. I was talking to some friends of mine about you and we were talking about how cute you were—are—and they asked me if you had a girlfriend. When I said no, they asked me why not? I didn't know the reason and then they said you must be gay. Of course they were kidding but it made me wonder and I've been wondering ever since. Are you sure this is what you want?" Mo asked.

"It's not what I want, Mo. It is what I am. I've worried and fretted over this too long and I just now understand it. That's why Eric and I have been hanging out so much. I couldn't have done this without his help." Matt responded.

"What are you saying? He made you gay?" Mo asked.

"No! Don't be ridiculous. No one can make you gay. I mean he has helped me understand my feelings and helped me accept who I am. I've come to realize that I don't have a choice; that it doesn't matter whether or not I want it. It is what I am and I am so tired of hiding things from you." Matt answered.

"Hiding things? From me? Like what?" Maureen interrogated.

"Well, just where I've been going out and who I've been seeing," Matt replied.

"What do you mean, who you've been seeing? Don't tell me you have a boyfriend! If you have a boyfriend and I still don't? I'm going to be pissed Matthew Michael!" she said.

"Don't get all excited! I don't have a boyfriend. I just meant that I've been going out with Eric—not as a couple but as friends. Of course, I did have a one night stand that I was dying to tell you about, but couldn't," Matt confessed.

"Are you kidding? A one night stand? How sleazy Matt!" Mo badgered.

"Forget about that. Are you okay with this? With me being gay?" Matt asked.

"Of course I am Matt. You are my friend. You are my best friend. You will always be my best friend. We've been through so much together and I'll always be there for you, no matter what. Just because you are gay doesn't mean that you've changed. You are still the wonderful person I've grown to know and love," Mo reassured him.

Tears fell down Matt's cheeks.

"Why are you crying?" Maureen asked, "I figured you would be happy, not sad."

"I am. I'm crying because I feel so relieved. You can't imagine how much this has been weighing on me. I can't believe how terrific you are. I don't think I've cried tears of joy until this very moment. You are the greatest friend a man could have. I love you," Matt said.

"I love you, too," Mo said, "We have so much to talk about. Why don't you come up for a night cap?"

"I'd love to," Matt agreed.

They opened a bottle of wine and talked until the sun came up. They shared tears and laughter and fears. Matt told her how bad he felt about hiding things from her and wanted her to share in his life, his entire life. It was the first time that Matt felt like he was living one complete life. Maureen knew about him being gay and could now share in that part of his life. He knew she would have to be introduced into it slowly however, but he knew she would be able to handle it. After all, she already liked Eric, one of his good friends and his only gay friend. The next several months they hung out in straight clubs and gay clubs. Eric was even willing to go to a straight club every now and again. "You never know where you might meet the man of your dreams," he always said.

Mo went along with them occasionally whenever they visited the gay bars, although she was one of the few women in the crowd.

Chapter 6

"It Can Happen"

"Happy New Year!" Eric approached Matt with a glass of champagne and cheered him. "So, any resolutions for 1985, Matt?"

"Not specifically. It's hard to come up with a resolution when you're already perfect like me!" He laughed.

Eric chuckled as well. "I'm sure you can think of something! If you think hard enough!"

"I can tell you my resolution this year is to find a man. Oh, wait. Wasn't that my resolution last year?" Mo chimed in.

"That wasn't your resolution, it was your wish!" Matt laughed. He had several glasses of bubbly and was feeling no pain.

"I don't know what you're talking about. You're just as single as I am!" Mo said.

"I guess I am, aren't I? Well, maybe that's both of our wishes or resolutions then." Matt held up his glass to cheer with Mo and Eric.

"I guess we're all in the same boat? Hey, I have an idea? Wanna make a bet?" Eric looked at Mo and Matt and raised his left eyebrow.

"What kind of bet?" Mo and Matt said in unison.

"Let's bet to see who gets a boyfriend first this year," Eric proposed.

"Alright. I say it will be me." Matt said.

"I say it's going to be me," Eric said.

"I think will be Matt." Mo said.

Eric laughed. "Why do you say that? Why don't you think you might find a boyfriend first, Maureen?"

"I just don't. That's all. I'm not saying I won't. The bet was about who will find a boyfriend *first*."

It was now the first of February and Mo was complaining about not having anyone again for St. Valentines' Day.

Matt was tired of her complaining again about being single this time of year and snapped at her, "Will you get over it? When was the last time you had a date for Valentine's Day?"

"What do you mean?" she asked.

"Have you ever had a Valentine's Day date? Not that I can remember, so why is this year any different?" Matt stated angrily.

"You don't have to be so mean about it. I can't help it. It's the most romantic day of the year and I am so sick of being alone every year," she said.

"Well I'm tired of you bitching about it every year. Aren't you?" He asked rather hastily.

"I'm just saying it sucks to be alone, geez!" She replied, getting annoyed with him.

"What do you mean alone? Haven't we always done something? What am I, chopped liver?"

"I would hardly call our going out to dinner a date, Matt!"

"I think you should think about how lucky you are to have friends. Boyfriends will come and go, but friends are here forever."

"I think the saying is that friends will come and go, but you will always have your family."

"I don't really care what the saying is. The fact is that I think you discount our friendship."

"Matt, how can you say that? You know how much I treasure our friendship. We've been through so much together. Maybe I've just gotten accustomed to saying whatever it is that I'm feeling and I no longer sugarcoat it anymore. I'm sorry. You know I love you and you know how happy I am that we're friends. Maybe I've lost perspective a little."

"Ah, don't worry about it. Part of me agrees with you. I guess that's why I don't like hearing it. It is the most romantic day of the year and as much as I would like to believe what I said and think that our friendship is enough, we both know it's not. I'm just angry because I'm tired of not having a boyfriend, too. I'm sorry."

"That's alright Matt. I'm used to your bitchiness by now!" She quipped.

He laughed. "Hey now!"

Matt thought about it. He thought about how nice it would be to have a boyfriend, to experience love with another man, but he didn't think it was within his control. He would just have to wait to find out what God had in store for him. What would the year bring? He was out to his best friend and he felt like a new man, but would he come out to his mother? He thought about it and didn't know how he could ever tell her. He thought it might be better to tell her when he found a boyfriend, that way he would be more comfortable about it and there would be a reason for it. He could take him home with him for Easter or Christmas, or any of the holidays. He closed his eyes and fantasized about how terrific that would be, how romantic it would be.

It was May and Matt was out to lunch with another friend from work. Dina was an administrative assistant that supported his department. She was hilarious. She had the quirkiest sense of humor and was always making Matt laugh. She wanted Matt to meet her sister, Caroline.

"Is she as crazy as you?"

"What do you mean crazy? Are you calling me a loo-loo bell? I ain't crazy you jack ass fool and neither am I!"

"I said crazy, not schizophrenic!" Matt laughed.

Dina was always playing a role, whether or not she was in a play. She always broke into some character to get a laugh. It always worked. She had Matt laughing so hard he thought he was going to piss his pants. She was an actress when she wasn't working for the firm and was very colorful and animated. She loved to make people laugh and had a knack of turning any conversation into something funny.

"My sissy ain't crazy. She's just goofy. Actually, she said that she was bringing a friend from work, too."

"What kind of friend? She's not dipping into the company ink is she? You know, fishing off of the company pier?"

Dina laughed. "I don't think so. She said it was a guy and besides, my sister's a lesbian."

"Oh, sorry."

"Sorry for what? Because she's a lesbian?"

"No! I guess I don't know what I meant. It just seemed like I should apologize."

They met at Pizzeria Uno downtown. As they approached the restaurant, Matt saw a guy standing there with a woman. He was gorgeous! He was a little taller than Matt, probably six feet two or three. Thinner than Matt, he probably only weighed a hundred and sixty pounds. He was clean shaven and looked like he had the smoothest skin. His hair was short, black and shiny. He had a smile that was so genuine and kind. Matt suddenly realized that he was staring at him and turned away to look back at Dina. The man smiled as Matt turned away.

As they got closer to the doors, Dina saw her sister. She had just arrived and was giving the hostess her name. Matt looked around to see who Caroline brought for lunch. What did he look like? Was he gay? If he was, was he cute? Caroline interrupted Matt's thoughts and said.

"Let's wait outside, in the sun." They walked outside.

"Matt, this is my sister, Caroline."

Caroline smiled and shook Matt's hand. "This is my friend Alan."

Matt looked up to see the man that he had been admiring from afar. He felt embarrassed and his cheeks turned a bit red as he grinned.

"It's nice to meet you," he said.

"It's nice to meet you, Matt." Alan stared into Matt's eyes, making him nervous.

They spent their lunch laughing and listening to stories of the two sisters from when they were younger. Matt couldn't tell how much of their stories was true and how much was fabricated. Matt and Alan kidded with Dina and Caroline, as well as each other. Matt was surprised that he and Alan got along so well.

Dina couldn't wait for them to get back to the office when she asked, "so, did you like him? Did you think he was cute? You two sure did seem to hit it off pretty good!" She nudged him.

"Yeah, I did. I thought he was really cute."

"So did you ask him out?"

"What? No. I didn't know if he was seeing someone or if he is even interested in me."

"What were you waiting for, an invitation?"

"I don't know. I'm new to this whole thing."

"Oh please, you've never asked anyone out? I find that hard to believe! I think you're just afraid of rejection!"

"I am not. I just didn't know how to read our encounter, that's all."

"Come on Matt. He liked you. Even I could tell that! Do you want me to call my sister and ask her what he said? I know they're talking about the same thing!"

"Only if it comes up in conversation!" Matt laughed. They both knew he really wanted to find out more about Alan.

Later that day, Matt was getting a report off of the printer that was near Dina's desk when she called him over. She was on the phone.

He walked up to her desk and motioned with his hands to her as if to say, "what?" Why would she want to talk to him if she was on the phone?

"Here." She handed him the phone.

"What? Who is it?"

"It's my sister. She wanted to know what you thought about Alan. I told her that you wanted to ask him out."

"You what? How could you?" Matt pressed the phone to his ear, "Hello?"

"Hi Matt. It's Caroline. So what did you think of Alan?"

"You get right to the point, don't you?"

"Life's too short to pussy-foot around with something you want. If you see something or someone you like, you have to go for it. So, did you like him? It seemed like you did."

"Yes, he's nice. I liked him. I was surprised at how well we got along, considering we only knew each other for less than an hour."

"So did you want to ask him out?"

"Again, straight to the point, huh? Well, I don't know. Is he seeing anyone?"

"No. Hold on." Caroline put him on hold.

Matt didn't know what to do. He wanted to hang up the phone and then make up some excuse as to what happened but knew it would be rude. Maybe he could say that he had another call and had to go. What was her sister going to ask next?

"Hello?" he heard on the other line. It was a familiar voice. Matt stood over Dina's desk and was worried that someone would overhear. He wanted to hang up the phone. He didn't know what to say.

"Oh…uh…Hi…Alan?"

"Yeah. Matt?"

"Yeah. Hey, thanks for lunch. I mean for meeting us there. I had fun." Matt felt embarrassed and could tell he was coming off foolishly.

"Yeah, me too."

"So…I was wondering…Would you like to go out sometime?" Matt knew he sounded like a little school boy asking the girl he had a crush on for a date. He wanted to sound a little smarter, a little more mature, but didn't know what that sounded like.

"Sure. I'd like that. How about this Saturday?"

"Oh…okay."

"Alright then. Let me give my number over here and at home and we can figure out what we want to do and where we'd like to go."

"That sounds like a plan." Matt hung up the phone and turned to Dina.

"So what did he say? Sounds like you have a date."

"Yeah, that wasn't so hard."

"Not with all that pushing and prodding," Dina said.

Matt showed up at Alan's at six o'clock Saturday. Alan opened the door and greeted Matt with a hug and a kiss. Matt was surprised by his forwardness but liked it. Alan said that he wanted to take Matt to a place that he loved and hadn't been in some time. He said that he thought and hoped that Matt would like it. Matt suggested that they go to dinner afterwards and that he would pick the restaurant. The plan sounded fine to Matt as he didn't know what he wanted to do and was fretting over his first real date with another man.

They spent the early evening at the cliffs near the Cliffhouse. Alan showed Matt where the ruins of the Sutro baths were and they took in the awesome view of the sun setting. Matt stood against the half-wall at the edge of the cliff that looked out over the water.

Alan walked towards Matt and stood behind him. He hugged him and placed his head over Matt's left shoulder and whispered, "Isn't it beautiful. I just love it here. There's something about the ocean."

"I do love it. I haven't been to the ocean in a very long time and had forgotten how much I missed it."

"Look right out there. Do you see it?" inquired Alan.

"I don't think so. What are you talking about?" Matt struggled to see what it was that Alan was referring to.

"The rocks out there." Alan pointed to a rock formation about a quarter of a mile from the beach and approximately a hundred feet tall.

"Yeah, I see it. Why?" Matt said.

"Look right in the center of it, what do you see?" Alan asked.

In the middle of the rock formation was a hole in the shape of a heart. "Oh, wow. I didn't notice that. How cool," Matt responded.

"I know. I love it. I like to visualize taking my worries and sending them through that hole and releasing them to the universe. What comes back is nothing but pure, positive energy and emotion." Alan's face was calm and tranquil.

At first Matt thought it was kind of a weird perspective but it seemed to work for Alan and if it benefited him, who was Matt to judge him?

"That's a nice thought," Matt said.

"Try it. I guarantee you will feel better," Alan suggested.

Matt focused on his breathing and visualized sending his frustrations out through the heart-shaped hole. When he inhaled he imagined that the energy coming back was love and a sense of peace.

Matt turned around and was now facing Alan. Alan still had his hands around Matt's waist. Matt continued, "Thanks for bringing me here and showing me this."

Alan moved and pressed his lips against Matt's. When he noticed that Matt didn't flinch, Alan looked at Matt, smiled, and kissed him again. This time, it was a long passionate kiss. As their kiss grew stronger, so did Alan's grip around Matt's torso. They were intertwined and Matt was getting excited. Alan's hands made their way from Matt's waist to his upper back and then to his head. Matt was somewhat embarrassed. He didn't know what others would say or how they would react if they saw them kissing or hugging each other. Matt wanted to stay there longer and enjoy Alan's kisses but they wouldn't be alone and he didn't want to put on a show for others to see.

Matt didn't like public displays of affection and disliked seeing others kissing and carrying on in public. He didn't like the fact that it was alright for a straight couple to make out in public but that it was unacceptable for a gay couple to do so. He didn't like it that a straight couple could hold hands without anyone saying anything or staring at them, yet when a gay couple held hands, they were stared at. It wasn't fair, but that's why he liked the Castro district so much. Maureen didn't understand this, although she was beginning to the more time she spent out in the Castro. Gay men and women were free to walk outdoors, hold hands or kiss on the streets without worrying what anyone thought or thinking that they were being watched. The Castro was so different than any other neighborhood in the City.

"The sun's almost down now. Maybe we should head back to the car and go to the restaurant."

"That sounds fine to me." Alan reached for Matt's hand.

It was so strange for Matt to be holding hands with someone, let alone another man. It seemed so natural for Alan. He didn't seem to worry in the least about what anyone would say, how anyone would react. Matt wished he felt this way as well. Matt released his hand from the warmth of Alan's to tie his shoe. Although his shoe strings didn't need adjusting, Matt thought it would be easier to use his shoe as an excuse than it would be to have a discussion around why he didn't want to hold Alan's hand. Alan didn't even notice that Matt's shoe wasn't untied.

They ate at the Sausage Factory. It was located in the heart of the gay district, on Castro Street, between eighteenth and nineteenth streets. Matt had the cannelloni and Alan had the lasagna. Alan was so easy going. They talked about their lunch and about how funny both Dina and Caroline were. They talked about the movies they had seen, the music they liked to listen to, and the television shows they loved to watch. Matt was surprised to find out that Alan wasn't an avid viewer of *Dallas, Dynasty, Knots Landing,* or *Falcon Crest*.

"Are you human? These are the best shows on television right now! I can't wait to watch them. I guess I'm just hooked. I can't believe you don't watch them," Matt said.

"I'm not a loyal fan, but I watch them every once in a while. Although I have to admit, I'm usually not home on Friday nights, so I don't get to see *Dallas* or *Falcon Crest*."

"That's too bad. *Falcon Crest* is my favorite show. It used to be *Dallas* until they killed off Bobby," Matt said seriously.

"You're too funny," laughed Alan.

They finished their dinner and debated on what to do next.

"Do you want to go out dancing or have some drinks somewhere?" Alan asked.

"Not really." Matt looked at Alan. He was grinning. "What's so funny?"

"I didn't really want to go out dancing or drinking, either. I just didn't want tonight to end. Do you want to go back to my place? We can just hang out there and chat."

"That sounds perfect." Matt grinned. For once, he didn't worry about what Alan was thinking or anticipating or whether or not he expected them to have sex. He was so comfortable with Alan; he just wanted to spend more time with him and knew he could handle the situation.

They spent hours kissing and fondling each other. They managed to discuss a second date, just before Matt decided to leave. It was two o'clock in the morning and Matt was tired.

"You can spend the night here, if you want? We don't have to do anything. I just thought you might be too tired to drive back home," Alan suggested.

"That's okay. Besides, it's not that far. I'll take a rain check, though." Matt thought about what a gentleman Alan was. For once, he had met someone who didn't want to jump in bed and have sex. Matt thought about Alan all the way home. Alan was the first guy to whom he was attracted physically, intellectually, and spiritually. Alan seemed to be very well grounded and content with his life. Matt liked the fact that Alan rarely got upset and remained calm, no matter the situation. Matt wanted to be less uptight and could learn something from Alan.

It had been a month since they first met and Alan and Matt were in bed, groping and fondling one another. It was the first time that Matt didn't have to think about what to do or how he should act. He was enjoying himself and felt extremely comfortable with Alan. That night was the first time that they had sex. Afterwards, Alan turned to Matt, "Well, how was that?"

Matt was flushed. "It was wonderful."

From that moment on, they fully enjoyed each other, in every aspect. They often spent the night at each other's apartments. His experiences with Alan were so new and pleasurable; Matt couldn't get enough of him. He felt as if he was addicted to sex and wanted to see Alan all the time. He couldn't help but to think about how many years he had wasted fighting against being gay and now he was finally free to feel like a real person in a real relationship. Sex had always scared him. He had tried it once, with a girl named Annabelle. She was so nice and pretty, but like his first girlfriend, something didn't feel right. When they were together their actions felt rehearsed; at least Matt's did. He started seeing Annabelle during his last year in high school. They dated for a little over three months when they decided to have sex. They had taken a long weekend trip down to San Diego and were staying in a hotel. They had a fun filled day in the sun and he was able to avoid sex the first night because of a sunburn. He knew he couldn't try the same excuse the next night. The second night, they decided to have sex. It ended with disastrous results and he never wanted to try it again. It was difficult for him to get hard and they argued when she brought the topic up or when she wanted to try it later.

"I just don't think it's the right time for me," he remembered saying.

"I think there's something else besides timing, Matt."

Annabelle got out of bed and sat on the chair, next to the little table adjacent to the bed. They argued about everything except Annabelle's suspicion that Matt might be gay.

They fought the next day and broke up when they returned home. Sex was scary. He had confirmed it. But now, it wasn't scary, not at all. He liked it. He liked Alan and how fulfilling their sex was together. "It wasn't scary. Not with the right person," he thought. He also thought it wasn't just a physical activity but mental as well. If one wasn't mentally into it, the sex wouldn't be as enjoyable or gratifying.

❦   ❦   ❦

He and Alan dated for four months before they broke up. Alan was insistent on telling Matt how much he loved him and Matt couldn't reciprocate. Matt knew he felt strong emotions for Alan, he just didn't know that it was love. He told him that he enjoyed him very much and that he still wanted to date, but he couldn't tell him that he loved him. Alan wanted a commitment.

Matt was extremely sad when they broke up. "I don't remember what I used to do before Alan," he told Eric.

"It's difficult, but maybe all you two need is a break from each other. It will allow you some time to find out how you really feel about him." Eric was good with advice although he was not good at listening to his own words of wisdom and was always looking for a boyfriend himself.

The day after he and Alan broke up, Matt lay in his bed, listening to music and crying because he didn't know what to do, who to call, or what to feel. He and Alan had become very close and spent most of their time together. The only thing he was sure of was the emptiness he now felt. He hoped that listening to Sade would help, but it only made matters worse. Sade had just released a new album that he and Alan listened to over and over. The words from *Sweetest Taboo* took on a different meaning now.

> "If I tell you,
> If I tell you now,
> Will you keep on,
> Will you keep on loving me.
> If I tell you,
> If I tell you how I feel,
> Will you keep bringing out the best in me."

Matt thought about the words and knew that Alan wouldn't be bringing out the best in him anymore. He hoped that his life wouldn't revert to the sadness he felt before he and Alan met.

It was only two months after they broke up when Matt heard that Alan was seeing someone else. His heart felt heavy. His stomach felt empty. Why was he jealous? Matt knew that he didn't particularly want to be with him, so why was he upset that he was already seeing someone else?

"I guess that' why they say, 'you always want what you can't have'?" Eric tried to console Matt.

Matt didn't let the disappointment stop him from dating. He continued to go out to bars with Eric and Mo. He dated several different individuals over the next year but nothing lasted more than three weeks.

One day, Eric approached him with the newspaper.

"Matt, didn't you go out with someone named Derek? Derek McDonald?"

"Yeah, why?"

"He was killed yesterday."

"Oh my God! How?"

"It says that they suspect the taxi driver of beating him to death. Did you know his friend, Joey Meyers?"

"Don't tell me Joey's dead, too?"

"No. He's just quoted in the paper."

"What's it say?" Matt reached out to grab the paper.

The article quoted Joey as saying he and Derek were taking a taxi home from the clubs and they were talking about some guys that they had met that night. Derek was speaking explicitly about some of the things that he wanted to do with one of the guys and Joey told him to be quiet. Joey was also quoted as saying that he felt uncomfortable talking about it because the cab driver seemed to be homophobic. He kept looking into his rear view mirror whenever Derek would say something crude. Joey tried to tell Derek to be quiet, but he continued.

Matt thought about it and totally understood. He and Derek had gone on a couple of dates, but Derek was too effeminate for Matt and was constantly saying whatever came to his mind, regardless of how it sounded. Matt knew after the second date that he couldn't date someone like that, but they agreed to be friends. Matt applied the "take home to mom test."

"If the guy isn't someone you feel comfortable taking home to introduce to your mother, you shouldn't be dating him," Eric advised.

Derek always told Matt that he was a "little too uptight" for him. It was somewhat of a joke with the two of them, considering that Derek was the complete opposite.

Matt continued reading the article in which Joey continued to talk about the minutes just before the taxi driver dropped him off at his apartment. He said that he and Derek had agreed to make their first stop Joey's apartment and then the taxi driver would proceed to take Derek to his apartment. Joey said that he gave Derek some money and told him to be careful. Derek reached over to give Joey a kiss as Joey got out of the taxi and closed the door.

"I just had an awful feeling when I closed the door and saw the taxi speed off," was Joey's last quote.

Four days later, Matt attended Derek's funeral. "It's just another example of how life is too short and you never know when you're going to die," Matt told Eric.

"How can you be so cold, Matt?"

"I'm not cold. I feel for him. I can't imagine what he went through during the last minutes of his life, but I've been to so many funerals, I think I'm just getting numb to them. Here today and gone tomorrow."

Eric shook his head. He couldn't understand Matt's point of view, probably because he wasn't acquainted with too many people who had died. His grandparents and parents were still living. He couldn't remember back to the last funeral he had attended.

The next day a follow-up article was in the paper telling the story of how the taxi driver pulled over onto the side of the street and ordered Derek to get out. Derek had gotten smart with the taxi driver and the next thing the driver knew was that he was hitting him. "I can't stand fags," he was quoted as saying, "and this one just pushed me over the edge, I guess." The driver knew there was no way he could cover it up and confessed to beating him and kicking him. After the beating, the driver left Derek on the side of the street. He didn't realize he was dead until he saw the paper the next day. He said that his wife had talked him into coming forward and confessing to the beating.

CHAPTER 7

"Deeper and Deeper"

It had been a year since Matt and Alan had split. As time passed, he realized that it was a good thing that they weren't seeing each other. He and Alan got along well but Alan was very laid back and wasn't as motivated as Matt. Although it was a nice balance, it somewhat annoyed Matt. He spent the next year and a half concentrating on his career and moving through the ranks at the firm. He was more successful and was earning respect from several different executives for some of the improvements he helped implement. After dating several individuals, he met Russell. He and Eric had been out at a restaurant in the Castro and Eric had noticed Russell staring over at their table. At first Eric thought he was staring at him and then realized that it was Matt that was the object of his eye.

Eric winked at Matt. "I think you have an admirer."

"What are you talking about?" Matt looked around the room and saw Russell staring at him, smiling. Matt smiled back.

After their dinner, Matt stepped outside and waited for Eric while he visited the restroom to rid himself of the many glasses of ice tea he had drunk. Russell walked outside and struck up a conversation with Matt, ending it with his phone number. Russell was just under six feet tall and had blonde hair. He didn't have the swimmer's body that Alan had and was a little overweight. His eyes were shockingly blue, almost hypnotic. He was wearing Tommy Hilfiger khakis and a blue, Ralph Lauren polo shirt that brought out his eyes even more. Russell was very much into appearances and materialism. He only shopped at the fanciest stores and only bought designer clothes. To Russell, it didn't matter what someone wore, it was who they wore. He mocked others who couldn't afford the finer things in life. This bothered Matt a lot. After they had been seeing each other for two months, Matt tried to break up with him. They got into a huge screaming match about how it was all Matt's fault and that he wasn't giving the relationship his all. Russell told Matt that he had been doing everything for the relationship and really, really wanted them to stay together. Matt expressed his concerns and decided to give him a second chance. After all, he did realize that he wasn't giving a hundred percent to the relationship and that maybe he needed to commit to the relationship instead of just throwing in the towel. Two months later, Matt ended the relationship after it was obvious that Russell wasn't going to change. Russell expected Matt to listen to his advice and to change, however, Russell wasn't making any sacrifices, thinking he was already perfect.

"This time, your guilt trip isn't going to work," Matt told him during a heated discussion as they were about to break up. They argued for close to two hours when Matt finally said he needed to go and he walked out.

"Goodbye." Matt didn't look back as he walked towards the door because he knew Russell was going to have a sad look on his face that might make Matt feel sorry for him. The breakup upset Matt because he wanted it to be non-confrontational and was hoping that they could remain friends. He was hoping they could at least act civilized when they saw each other. Unfortunately, Russell was bitter and held a grudge against Matt for dumping him.

After meeting Adam, Matt looked back at his relationship with Russell and wondered what he was thinking to stay in that relationship for as long as he did. Adam was half Nicaraguan and half American. He looked almost Asian with slightly-slanted eyes. His dark skin was smooth and made him look like he was only twenty rather than twenty-six. When he smiled, dimples appeared on his cheeks. His eyes were brown; however Adam wore blue contacts to conceal them. Adam was a programmer for another investment banking firm and they had met at a bar, of all places. As much preaching as Matt did to Eric about how he was never going to meet anyone of any quality at a bar, Matt had to apologize and promise that he would never say that again. Although it wasn't strange for Matt to meet someone in a bar, it was strange that Matt had a strong feeling that he was going to meet someone the night he went out.

It was early December, 1988 and Matt had been out Christmas shopping and had a very successful day. He decided to go out that night by himself to celebrate his rewarding day. As much as he liked spending time with Eric, Matt was getting tired of him always pointing out guys he thought were cute but unapproachable. Eric spent more time ogling guys than talking to Matt. Tonight would be different. Matt decided what he really wanted was to enjoy the evening and music and have fun.

His plan was to stay out for a short bit and then go home. There was something about that day that he couldn't shake. It was as if every planet was in perfect alignment and that for some reason, he felt this enormous amount of energy and felt like he had this golden light emanating out of his body. Maybe it was his aura. Whatever it was, he was in a great mood and knew people could sense there was something about him that night. He had a couple of drinks and was enjoying the music when he heard the dance mix to *Like a Virgin*. This was his favorite song at the time and he couldn't help but run to the dance floor to start dancing.

The one thing different between a gay bar and a straight bar is that you can dance by yourself and no one thinks any differently of you. Usually the dance floors were so crowded; no one knew you were dancing alone anyway. He made it half way through the song when all of a sudden he saw this man smiling at him and moving over to dance with him. It looked like he was with a couple of friends who may have been a couple. He moved closer and closer until the next song, *Everything She Wants* came on. It didn't matter what *Wham!* or George Michael sang, Matt would have a smile on his face and would be seen dancing to it. He was soon dancing with this cute boy who couldn't stop smiling. They danced together the rest of the night. They took a break to introduce themselves to each other and talk a little but then went back on the dance floor. Their chemistry was incredible. Matt was surprised that this extremely cute guy was actually dancing with him, flirting with him. As the dance floor got even more crowded, the space between them shortened and they were soon in each other's face. It didn't take long for Adam to turn to Matt and kiss him. It was one of those nights when you couldn't just stop at one kiss. Towards the end of the evening, Matt remembered, they were kissing more than they were dancing. Adam spent the night at Matt's because he didn't live in the city, but they didn't have sex.

They spent the next entire day together. First they woke up late, which was something that Matt never did on the weekends, and cuddled in bed. Matt remembered being so comfortable that he never wanted to leave because he thought it was too good to be true. He was worried that for some reason when they got up it would all go away, as if it were a dream. They showered together and went shopping and ate at a cute little restaurant in Noe Valley.

They began dating and were soon falling in love, really in love. When Matt looked back to his other relationships, he thought about what they had meant and what they had provided him. His relationship with Alan showed him that he didn't always need to be serious and driven. One should maintain a balance between determination and patience. The result would be contentment. His relationship with Russell taught him that he wasn't perfect and that he needed to take the other person's feelings and character into consideration at all times. He hoped he wouldn't have to look back at his and Adam's relationship to find out what he needed to learn.

Matt always said, "You should always take something away from a relationship. Some lesson that you can apply to the next."

Matt's longest relationship had only been five months, so he was hoping that if he and Adam could make it that long; they might be able to stay together for quite a while. They did. They spent time together riding bikes, watching movies, shopping, playing games with their friends, and cooking. Adam didn't like to cook but loved to help Matt in the kitchen. Adam would chop all the ingredients for the recipe while Matt cooked the food. Adam also took responsibility for cleaning the kitchen and all the dishes. Matt loved him for this as he hated doing two things, dishes and laundry. He couldn't convince Adam to do his laundry, but that was okay. They took turns staying over at each other's apartments during the weekends. Matt hated Sunday evenings because he knew that Adam would go home and he'd be alone Monday night. He was getting used to having Adam in his bed and didn't like the idea of being without him. The time they spent together was fabulous. They never fought and got along with each other's friends so well, it was difficult for people to figure out who was friends with whom first. After a year and a half of dating, Matt asked Adam to move in with him. Adam told him that he wanted to but that he wasn't sure it was the right time for him to do so. Adam hadn't told his parents he was gay and knew that this would be something they questioned. By not moving in with Matt, he could avoid the confrontation for a while longer. Matt tried to convince him that it would be great and that they could still have their independence, but Adam wouldn't.

During the next six months, Adam began to go out during the week without Matt and would come over to Matt's on Friday night tired from going out the previous night. Matt didn't like this but he didn't want to put restrictions on what Adam could do, so he remained quiet. Their once strong relationship began to weaken. Adam became more and more withdrawn as if something was bothering him. Matt wanted to ask him what was wrong, but figured that if he wanted to discuss it, he would. Matt was soon dissatisfied with their relationship and no longer looked at Adam as he once did. The chemistry that they shared had dissipated and their sexual attraction to each other was also diminishing. Just after their two year anniversary, Adam told Matt that he didn't want to see him anymore. Matt was relieved and disappointed at the same time. He wanted them to work on their relationship but knew that it would take both of them to talk through their problems and he didn't think Adam was interested in that as an option. They decided not to see each other and within two weeks, Adam was seeing someone else.

"I can't believe it!" Matt was dumbfounded when Eric told him that he saw Adam out with someone else, kissing him. "That son of a bitch!"

"I didn't want to tell you. I'm sorry, but I thought you might find out sooner or later and you may as well hear it from a friend." Eric had contemplated on whether to tell Matt the news and was hoping he wouldn't take it so hard.

Matt had been talking about how glad he was that they weren't seeing each other anymore and was happy to finally do some things that he wanted to do that he couldn't do when he was with Adam. "I just can't believe that snake! He was probably seeing him before we even broke up!"

"I wouldn't go that far, Matt."

"Why not? It's only been two weeks? He sure isn't acting like someone who wanted to take some time off from seeing each other. For God's sake, we were together for two years and just like that he can run to someone else?" Matt snapped his fingers in disgust.

"I don't know what to tell you."

"You don't have to say anything. I don't care. Fuck him! He can go to hell!"

Matt didn't shed a tear while he was at Eric's. On his way home, he cried like he'd never cried before. Why did Adam have to do such a thing? Why did he care so much? Matt thought about what it meant. If Adam could find a replacement so easily, it meant that their relationship wasn't as special as he thought. "God, he's probably already in love with him!" he thought.

Although Matt had been putting on a front that everything was okay, he missed Adam. He missed having someone share his bed. He missed having someone with him during the weekends. He missed having someone to cuddle with during the cold, San Francisco evenings. He missed the scent of Adam and how he kissed him. He hated that he was so upset. He hated that he was crying. He hated feeling like he wasn't in control of his emotions. He hated that he wanted to vomit. He hated Adam.

Adam tried calling him a couple of times. Matt hung up on him each time. Finally, one day at work Adam got through.

"Listen Adam, I don't know what you want, but leave me alone."

"Why are you so upset? I don't know why you won't talk to me?" Adam asked.

"Oh, I don't know. Why don't you tell me what you've been up to?" Matt decided to see if Adam would tell him about his new boyfriend. Adam went on to tell him what he had been doing, never mentioning that he was seeing someone else.

"Do you take me for a fool?" Matt asked.

"No, why?"

"I know you're seeing someone else already. I don't know how you can and then call me like nothing's changed," Matt barked.

"I thought you were just as comfortable as I was about our breaking up?" Adam professed.

"I was. I mean, I am. I just can't believe you are seeing someone else. So soon."

"What's the big deal? I'm sure you haven't been sitting around doing nothing?"

"You just don't get it. That's why I don't want to talk to you," Matt argued.

"So that's it? That's all you have to say to me?" Adam pleaded.

"No. One more thing. You didn't even want to talk about our problems. All you wanted to do was to leave. Answer this, were you seeing him before we broke up?"

"What? No. I can't believe you think I would do that to you," Adam stated.

"I don't believe you," Matt said, feeling the resentment growing inside him.

"Well, I wouldn't lie. You should know that."

"You'd think I could believe you after all these years, but I don't. And that speaks for itself!" Matt hung up the phone.

As angry as Matt was at Adam, he was still feeling for him. The nights were the worst. He tried to keep himself busy and began putting in more and more hours at work. He went to bed and cried. It was so quiet in his apartment and it felt so lonely. He knew that he needed to go out and meet someone else. That would help him get over Adam, but he just wasn't interested in doing that. He couldn't stop thinking about Adam. They had such an emotional connection and he missed it. He thought they would be together forever and that Adam was his soul mate. How could he be so wrong? Maybe Adam wasn't his soul mate, after all. Maybe it was just Matt's imagination.

Eric kept trying to drag Matt out to meet a new man but he didn't want to go. When he did go out, he didn't enjoy himself. There was something humiliating about going out and looking for love.

"Maybe I'm just a romantic but I think I'll find it when I'm supposed to," Matt told Eric.

"Who are you going to meet in your apartment?"

"No one, but going out doesn't seem to get me anywhere, either."

"Matt, isn't that where you met Adam?"

"My point exactly!"

"I can tell I'm not going to get anywhere, am I?" Eric relinquished.

It was a difficult time for him. Although he knew that it was over between him and Adam, he couldn't help but think back to the times that they had spent together and how much he still loved him.

Two years later, Maureen was moving into a new house. She was making good money and was the first one of them from school to make the leap to home ownership. Matt was too worried about what he was going to buy her for her housewarming to worry about whether or not he would meet anyone. He wasn't interested in meeting anyone. Maybe he was getting older. He hoped he wasn't getting bitter. When he walked into the house, he couldn't believe the transformation that Mo made from when he first saw it with her when she was deciding on whether to buy it. As he looked for her so he could tell her how wonderful her place was, he saw him. Standing there against the fireplace, the man looked so cute. Matt remembered thinking that he was the kind of guy that he could go out with, should go out with. Then they were introduced and Matt found out a little bit more about him. He was a doctor. That wasn't so appealing, knowing the kind of hours they kept but it didn't matter. Matt felt his heart beating for the first time in a long while and he liked it.

Their first date was to the San Francisco Symphony. Matt hadn't gotten around to attending an event there but always wanted to. He suggested they go there. When he showed up at Ryan's house, he couldn't believe how incredibly gorgeous Ryan looked. Matt thought he must be crazy to think that Ryan would want him. They enjoyed the symphony and spent the rest of the evening talking about themselves over coffee. Matt was somewhat surprised at the end of their coffee when Ryan reached over and grabbed his hand that was resting on the table.

"Would you mind if I called you sometime?" Ryan asked.

"I'd love it," Matt thought his response was a little eager and decided to tone it down somewhat. "I mean, I've had a great evening and it has been so nice to be able to sit down and talk about anything and everything. I don't think we had an awkward pause the whole evening."

"I'd have to agree. I've really enjoyed myself, too. This date was quite different than the last one I was on," Ryan replied.

"My date didn't have anything to talk about and just sat at the table over dinner. I thought I was going to scream. He didn't laugh at any of my jokes. I don't think he changed his expression once. You may think this is awful, but I called my friend and told her to page me in 10 minutes. So I went back to the table and choked down the rest of my dinner. I think it was veal scaloppini, and it was as dry as he was! Anyway, my friend paged me and I then had the excuse I needed to leave. I felt bad but I was relieved to end that night! I'm sure he wasn't upset since he didn't seem to be enjoying himself either." Ryan looked up at Matt, waiting for some kind of acceptance that what he had done was perfectly fine.

"I guess I'll have to wait and see if you ever get paged when we are out then," cracked Matt.

"I doubt that will happen, unless it's a real emergency," replied Ryan, smiling.

"We all have our little tricks and games we have to play now and again, don't we?" Matt winked with one eye, making Ryan chuckle.

Ryan and Matt began dating for a month when Ryan told him that he wasn't planning on seeing anyone else and wanted to know what Matt thought.

"I was already thinking that myself but I didn't want to mention it. I thought it might be too early in our relationship," Matt said.

"Oh, good. I'm relieved. I thought the same thing but then I didn't want to leave anything to chance. I have to tell you Matt, this last month has been the happiest I've seen in quite a long time." Ryan gazed at Matt.

"Me, too." Matt was smiling. "Hey Ryan, how would you like to go to New York with me?"

"When? You know my schedule is pretty crazy, but if I have enough time in advance to plan it, I would love to go. The last time I was there was when I was a little boy so I don't remember too much."

"I have to attend this training session in early November and I was going to make a long weekend out of it but thought it would be much more fun if you joined me." Matt was hoping that Ryan would be able to get the time off and join him, otherwise it wouldn't be much fun. Matt didn't like taking vacations or sight-seeing by himself. It was always much more fun with someone else. Ordinarily he would invite Mo but now that he was dating this terrific guy, he thought about how wonderfully romantic the trip could be. Although Mo was always a lot of fun when they vacationed together, he often found himself thinking how terrific it would be if he was on the trip with a lover.

"I'll check my schedule, but I'm sure it won't be a problem. There are a couple of months before the trip so I'll check to see who'll be on staff to take care of my patients."

Ryan and Matt flew into La Guardia on a Friday night, arrived at their hotel, unpacked their luggage, and headed out for some fun.

"Do you want to get a bite to eat?" Ryan asked. He hadn't eaten anything except for the dinner they served aboard the flight and it left him unsatisfied.

"That's a good idea. Do you want to get something light and then head to a bar or club?" Matt questioned.

"Sure. I just want something quick and easy that will satisfy me," Ryan answered.

"I wish you would have told me that when we were back at the hotel. I would have planned a different evening," Matt gushed teasingly.

"Behave! There's plenty of time for that," Ryan said, gently placing his arm around Matt's shoulders. Matt pulled away. He was still uncomfortable with displaying affection in public, especially when he was in an unfamiliar city and unsure about the neighborhood and how they would accept a gay couple walking down the street.

"Is there something wrong?" Ryan questioned.

"No, not a thing. Hey, what about pizza? We should have authentic New York pizza while we're here. We can have a good dinner tomorrow night," Matt suggested.

"Perfect! It has to be better than that chicken we had on the plane. That was awful! Do they ever think to actually add some flavor to their meals?" Ryan asked.

"Apparently not," Matt joked.

The next day they spent touring the city. They climbed the Statue of Liberty, rode to the top of the Empire State Building, and visited Greenwich Village. When they returned to Midtown, they decided to see a play. All the talk on Broadway was about the musical, *Crazy for You*. It was a remake of the 1930's Gershwin musical *Girl Crazy* and was nominated for nine Tony Awards, including Best Musical. *Crazy for You* was the story of Bobby Child, a well-to-do 1930's playboy, whose dream in life was to dance despite the serious efforts of his mother and soon-to-be-ex-fiancée. The advertisements made it very appealing by calling it a "high energy comedy which includes mistaken identity, plot twists, fabulous dance numbers and classic Gershwin music." Although Matt didn't enjoy musicals as much as he did comedic or dramatic plays, Ryan really wanted to see it.

"Just think, if it wins the Tony, we can say we saw it," quipped Ryan.

"We can also see *Two Trains Running*, it's nominated for Best Play," responded Matt.

"It doesn't sound that good though. Let's just see *Crazy for You*. I think it's perfect." Ryan winked.

"How can I disagree with that?" Matt retorted.

That evening, they enjoyed Fettuccine Alfredo, Chicken Saltimbocca, tiramisu, and a bottle of Chianti at Vita Buona, a charming little restaurant tucked away below one of the apartment buildings on 48th Avenue. During the play that night, Matt thought that it was a good idea that they decided to see a musical instead of the play he wanted to see. He was sure they would have slept through it after the heavy dinner and wine. The weekend went by quickly as soon they were headed back to California.

On the way back from New York, they discussed taking another trip. Ryan loved getting away and thought that they should plan their next trip to give him something to look forward to. He knew the next month would be extremely busy and that he would need motivation to get through the long hours that awaited him. Matt suggested that they plan a trip to Europe. He wanted to travel as his father had. He wanted to see as much as possible because he always thought life was too short and one never knew when it would all end. He had been to so many of his relative's and friend's funerals, old and young, that he knew in an instant one's life could change and what was held to be so dear could be gone forever. He was hell-bent on making sure that he lived his life to the fullest, that he experienced all there was to experience, and to make sure that everyone he appreciated knew it.

The following summer, they packed their bags and headed on to their seven country visit of Europe. Although they had been dating for close to a year, Matt was a little nervous not knowing how he and Ryan would get along being together for almost three weeks. Vacations had a tendency of testing relationships and friendships. For the first time in their relationship, Matt and Ryan were going to be living together. How would they get along? Would they get tired of listening to each other? Would they want to do the same things? Matt had planned the trip through a tour company and thought that either Ryan or he would get tired of riding in the tour bus all over Europe. He and Ryan had agreed that this was the best way to see Europe for the first time because they would be able to get a sampling of what each country had to offer. Ryan was hesitant to take such a long trip but Matt had begged and was so excited to go that he couldn't refuse. Ryan knew that when they returned he would have to make up all the time off and that he was going to have to cover the shifts of all the doctors he asked to fill in for him while he was gone. It wouldn't be fun when he returned so he thought he'd better make sure to live it up in Europe and to enjoy every minute of it. Ryan's perspective and attitude toward the trip was comforting to Matt who thought that maybe his worries about the trip were unsubstantiated.

Their first stop on their trip was in Brussels, Belgium where they enjoyed waffles in the morning and local beer in the afternoon. Brussels was rich with history and stories told by the local people. Matt couldn't help but wonder what kind of history he and Ryan might have but he tried not to think about it. He wanted to enjoy their time together and not worry about the future which is what he did.

As soon as they arrived in Munich, Germany, they headed to the pier where they took a cruise down the Rhine River. From their boat, they saw incredible castles along he mountainside lush with green vegetation. Several times Ryan moved closer to Matt to show him affection, but Matt withdrew. The other people on the tour were mostly older couples and Matt felt uncomfortable about displaying any affection. He didn't know whether the others knew he and Ryan were a couple or whether they thought they were just friends but he didn't want to give them any reason to make their trip uncomfortable. They were at the beginning of their journey with all these people and Matt didn't want the trip to be awkward for the duration. Besides, as he told Ryan, "There will be plenty of time for affection later." Matt could still sense that Ryan was disappointed and that he wanted to enjoy the romanticism of the moment. Matt hated feeling the way he did. He knew it shouldn't matter what anyone else thought about him or Ryan or their relationship but he didn't like confrontation or uneasy situations and sought to avoid them.

They made stops in Austria and Switzerland but the highlight of their trip was when they finally arrived in Venice. Ryan was in awe of the city, the canals, the magnificent architecture, and especially the wonderful people.

"I feel like I'm in a movie," Ryan glowed.

"What do you mean?" Matt questioned.

"This just feels unreal. It's like we are on a back lot somewhere in Hollywood or something. It's just incredible. Don't you think so?" Ryan continued to be captivated with the city.

"It's pretty nice," Matt replied.

"Pretty nice? This is the most romantic place on earth!" Ryan gushed.

"What's gotten into you?" Matt really liked Venice but wasn't as awe-struck as Ryan.

"I just love this weather and the sites and everything about this place. I wish we were staying somewhere here instead of in the city," said Ryan referring to their hotel which was further in the valley, away from Venice and the canals.

They went on a gondola ride where Ryan secretly placed his hand onto Matt's, hidden from site by his jacket that covered them. Matt's first reaction was to look around to see if anyone noticed. They were safe as everyone else in the gondola was busy looking at the laundry hanging from the clothes lines or the geraniums blooming in the window baskets high about their heads. Matt sighed and smiled at Ryan. He really wanted to kiss him and tell him how much in love he was but of course, he couldn't. Matt's eyes started to well up with tears.

"What's wrong?" Ryan asked, noticing the change in Matt's expression.

"Nothing. This really is incredible, that's all." Matt disguised his torment.

From Venice, they headed to Paris and Nice where they continued to fall in love with the cities, the people, the food, and each other. Their last stop on their tour was in Barcelona, Spain. Matt tried using the Spanish he had studied but soon found that it was much more difficult than he thought. He'd forgotten how rapidly the Spaniards spoke but was surprised by how much was coming back to him from those early years in school. Their first night there, Ryan had seen several older men sitting around one of the plazas, playing cards, laughing, and drinking from a leather-type flask in the shape of a kidney. When they returned to the hotel that night Ryan asked the concierge about it and he told him it was a "bota." The man went on to tell Ryan the rich history of Spain and how the bota had been around for centuries and was a means by which Spaniards could carry their wine which would last as long as it took them to drink it.

"It is very popular to have one of these," the man said, "it is a symbol of pleasant times, good company, and good cheer. Many of the tiendas sell them but you should look for one made by Las Tres Zetas. They have been making them for years and are the authentic botas. This is what you will want."

That was all Ryan needed to hear and the next day, they set out to find a place where he could buy his "bota." As they headed into the center of the plaza in the heart of town, Matt suggested they go away from the more touristy areas and down the alleys into the stores where most of the locals shopped.

Barcelona was a web of alleys with all kinds of shops down each one. There were shoe stores, liquor shops, bakeries, book stores, and restaurants, all tucked away. One turn down an alley led to another turn which led to another turn. Soon, they came across a shop that sold different kinds of leather goods, and low and behold, Ryan saw the bota for which he had been yearning.

As they walked out of the store, Matt and Ryan said simultaneously, "So, which way do we go?"

"I don't know. Don't you remember?" Matt responded.

"I was too busy looking in the shops and windows," Ryan replied

"I think we need to go this way and then at the end of this alley, we go right," Matt suggested.

"Are you sure?" Ryan questioned.

"Not really," Matt tried to remember something unique about one of the shops or alleys which would aid them in their quest to find their hotel.

After an hour of walking Ryan said, "This shop looks familiar, doesn't it?"

"I don't know. How can you tell? There are so many shoe stores and clothing shops, they all look alike." Matt started to show his concern. "I think we're lost."

"Come on, we can't be lost. This city isn't that big," Ryan said trying to reassure him.

"It wouldn't be bad if we could see out of this alley but I can't see a thing. No distinguishable buildings or landmarks of any kind," Matt said worriedly.

"Don't freak out, we'll figure this out." Ryan pulled out a map of the city and began studying it.

"Do you even know where we are?" Matt quipped.

"Not really," Ryan answered.

"Then the map isn't going to do you any good," Matt snapped.

"Well, do you have any ideas?" Ryan angrily replied.

At that moment a disheveled man approached them from one of the doorways ahead of them.

"Necesitas ayuda?" the man asked, wondering if they needed help.

"No, gracias," Matt replied.

"Pienso que usted necesita ayuda," the man answered, insisting that they needed help.

"No, pero gracias." Matt tried to be cordial although something within him was telling him that there was something wrong.

"Turistas perdidos. Qué tontos. Usted no puede necesitar ayuda ahora pero usted en un minuto. Usted me hace enfermo, maricones!" the man hollered as he approached them.

Matt picked up a bit of what the man was saying and knew that he had called them stupid and had said something about them needing help in a minute. Matt saw another man coming from the end of the alley, just behind the man who was now glaring at them. His heart was racing and he turned to look at Ryan whose face was inexpressive. As Ryan stood there puzzled, Matt whispered, "I think we should run Ryan."

"Why, what did he say?" Ryan questioned.

"It wasn't anything good," Matt pleaded.

The only thing Matt could envision was them being robbed and possibly beaten to death. Certainly they stood a chance against the one man but with his accomplice closing in behind him, they wouldn't stand a chance, especially since they were lost. Matt froze for a minute as he could hear his heart beating in his ears. What should he do? He quickly scanned the alley and saw there was no way out for them. They couldn't turn to run because there was a dead-end behind them. The only way out was to go directly at the begrudging old man headed right at them.

"Let's go Ryan," Matt said as he grabbed onto Ryan's arm and began walking toward the man.

"No deseamos cualquier problemas," Matt said, communicating to the man that they didn't want any problems.

As the man approached, he reached into his upper jacket. Matt's heart raced with fear. Was it a gun? A knife? Matt could barely swallow and feared he would pass out.

Just then, the man who Matt thought was the aggravated man's accomplice began yelling and screaming things that Matt couldn't understand. The only word he heard was "policia" and for that second, Matt felt that his prayer had been answered. The angered man was still approaching them and began to pull out something from his jacket when the other man began running in their direction and shouting. Matt and Ryan stood against the wall while the crazed man stopped, turned the opposite direction, and running away from them, knocked the other man over. He continued to run out of the alley.

As the man approached Matt and Ryan he said with a slight accent, "You have to be careful. What are you two doing down here?"

"We were out shopping and got a little lost I'm afraid," Ryan said. Matt was still shaking from the experience.

"Did he do anything?" The man asked.

"No, we're fine thanks to you. We're so glad you came when you did," Ryan replied.

"These alleys are safe during the day but at night, they are filled with free loaders wanting to knock over tourists. Poverty is quite high here in Barcelona."

The man went on to tell them how he was overseas working for his company in Spain and had been robbed the first month he was there.

"It really makes me angry when I see this. I feel like I have an obligation to help out when I see something like this. Maybe someone will look after me the next time something happens."

"Well, we really appreciate it." Ryan shook the man's hand. "Can we buy you a drink or take you to dinner or something?"

"You don't have to do that, but it would be nice to have dinner with someone other than myself for a change," the man smiled.

The man helped them find their way out of the alleys and back to their hotel where they changed and met him later for dinner. All the way back, Matt didn't say a word. When they got back to the hotel, Ryan said, "Matt, are you okay?"

"I'm fine. I just can't believe how I acted. I was so scared I couldn't do anything."

"It's alright. We're fine, we would have been fine and it's in the past now, don't dwell on it," Ryan said comfortingly.

"How can you say that? And how can you be so nonchalant about the whole thing? Weren't you worried to death? I thought we were going to be killed," Matt confessed, trying to get control of his emotions.

He continued, "I just feel so vulnerable now that I have you. I don't want to lose what we have and I certainly don't know what I'd do without you."

"You aren't going to lose me and yes, I was worried, but I didn't know what was going to happen. It all worked out okay and we are fine. Why don't you take a quick shower and then we can head out to the restaurant."

After a couple of bottles of wine that night, Matt was back to his old self and was enjoying himself again. They only had two days left of their vacation before their journey back home. The trip had been so wonderful, in so many ways, Matt thought.

❦   ❦   ❦

After all the fun, laughter, tears, and two years, they decided to move in together. Although Ryan made excellent money, he still had student loans from medical school that he was making payments on and was still living in a flat in the Marina district of town. His rent was outrageous. He was paying twenty-two-hundred-dollars a month for his two bedroom, one bath unit. When they decided to live together, Matt convinced him how much cheaper it would be for them to own rather than rent. Of course, a legal agreement would have to be created to make sure that they shared in the equity and tax savings. Matt was a romantic but he was also practical. They found a two bedroom, two bath house just off of Market Street, halfway up the hill towards Twin Peaks. The house was originally built in 1912 and had a lot of character. They decided to paint the crown molding white and the rest of the living room a coffee color. They would accent it with avocado colored drapes. The view from their living room was spectacular. It overlooked the bay and downtown. The lights at night were breath taking.

The day they moved in, Ryan went to one of the neighborhood liquor stores and contemplated on what to buy for almost an hour. He wanted the night to be special and one they would never forget. He looked at red wines but then thought a bottle of white might be more suitable. Then he decided that an ordinary bottle of white wine wouldn't be special enough and decided to look at champagnes. After spending almost a half an hour talking to the owner, he decided on the one hundred and fifty-dollar-bottle of Dom Perignon. Ryan placed the bottle on ice earlier in the evening when he met the movers at the house.

When he and Ryan got there that evening, Ryan hunted through the kitchen boxes to find the champagne flutes. The cork echoed against the naked walls when he popped open the bottle. After he poured two glasses, he proceeded to the living room where Matt was starting to unpack.

"Stop that right now," Ryan ordered.

Matt didn't even turn around but responded, "We may as well get a head start on this stuff."

"There will be plenty of time for that. This is more important," Ryan replied.

Matt turned around and noticed Ryan standing there with the glasses of champagne. "What's this?" he said.

"Some of the best champagne you and I will ever have." Ryan beamed.

"What is this?" Matt questioned.

"Some Dom Perignon for our new house and our new wonderful life together." Ryan held up his glass.

Matt held up his glass in return and that night they celebrated what would be the first day of the rest of their lives.

CHAPTER 8

"The Contract"

Matt and Ryan had been together for nearly five years and how time had flown. Still, it seemed like they were in as much love as when they first met that night at Maureen's. The three of them had been very close and frequently went out to find a boyfriend for Mo. Of course, they never succeeded. Mo was too particular. The prospects that Ryan and Matt picked out were either too short, too tall, too skinny, too fat, or too desperate looking. If the candidate managed to make it through the first round, she would put him through the second test of physical attributes. His hair was too long or it was too short or she didn't like men with blonde hair, but sometimes she did. She knew she hated redheads, however.

Maureen was now thirty-four and hadn't experienced a lot of men. She was still looking for the knight in shining armor to save her. The once happy and cheerful person Matt had known had turned into a bitter and depressed woman. She said she could hear her "maternal clock" ticking and that she wanted to have a baby soon, although she couldn't see herself as a single mother. She thought it would be too difficult to raise a child on her own, but someday, she thought, "I'll find my man and we will have children and live happily every after." It was this belief system that got in Mo's way. From Matt's perspective, she was too busy looking for the perfect mate instead of giving a guy a chance even though he might not meet all of her criteria. Matt would constantly remind her, "Happiness is not a destination; it's a way of travel." He had read this somewhere and always thought that this was the way one should live life.

One night while eating dinner at the China Court Cafe in the Castro district of San Francisco, Matt noticed a gay couple enter the restaurant with a child. The boy was about three years old and was dressed up in khaki pants and a polo shirt. Matt couldn't help but stare at the child and admire him. He always said if he had a child, he would be dressed just like that. For all intents and purposes, the little boy he was admiring could have been his child.

Ryan, obviously aware of Matt's lack of attention, grinned and said, "Matthew Michael Tylo, paging Matthew Michael Tylo." Matt laughed.

"I'm sorry, but look at him, isn't he just the cutest kid you've ever seen?"

Ryan grinned, showing off his perfectly straight and white teeth.

"Yes, he is. Wouldn't it be wonderful to have one of our own?"

"Are you serious? Do you mean it?" Matt replied excitedly.

"Well, to tell you the truth, I'm not sure what I meant," Ryan replied.

"Do you think you'd want to be a father? Do you want to raise a baby with me?" Matt asked.

"I know how much you love children and well, so do I." Matt could tell Ryan was thinking about it as he was talking. "But do you really want a child? That's a pretty big commitment," Ryan replied, not sure of what it was that *he* wanted.

"A commitment to what? Us or the child," asked Matt inquisitively.

Ryan looked up and into Matt's eyes.

"You know how I feel about you. You know I have no problem committing to you, to us, to this relationship. I was talking about the child."

Matt had a puzzled look on his face.

"This is going to require some thought, if you're serious, Ryan."

"I'm not sure whether I am or not, actually," Ryan retorted.

Just then, the waiter approached with the bill. Matt and Ryan settled it and went back to their place, after stopping off for ice cream which was a Sunday ritual. It symbolized the conclusion of their weekend. Ryan always said, "I can't start my Mondays off unless I have my double mocha scoop on Sunday night."

The two retired around ten o'clock and proceeded to make passionate love. There was something different about that night. There was a sense of extreme closeness that they hadn't felt since they first started dating. After making love, they held each other in their arms and drifted off to sleep.

It was about two o'clock in the morning when Ryan awakened, and turned to Matt.

"Are you awake? Honey, wake up."

"What? What's the matter?" Matt muttered, wondering what the sense of urgency was.

"I love you and I want to raise a child with you. Let's have a baby!" Ryan exclaimed with vigor.

Matt was now sitting upright on the bed.

"Are you serious?"

"Of course I am, how serious are you?" Ryan asked.

"I'm very serious. Let's do it. Let's have a child." Matt gave Ryan a long and passionate kiss. "Do you know what we need to do?"

"What do you mean what we need to do?" Ryan laughed.

"Do you have any idea what are next step should be?" Matt asked.

"I guess we have to think about whether we adopt or have a surrogate mother carry the baby." Ryan said.

"I'd rather have our own baby rather than adopt. Does that sound bad? I've just always dreamt of having a baby that had either my or my partner's genes," Matt replied.

"That's fine and I agree. I can bring home some information from my office and you can look it over. It details all our options," Ryan said.

"Okay, and I'll do some research on it at work today. There's also a woman I work with who looked into all the different options so I'll ask her. I'll let you know what I find out tonight. Oh, I can't wait!" Matt said excitedly.

"Alright, sounds awesome." Ryan sighed but couldn't get the grin off his face.

The alarm clock sounded and it was time for Ryan to get to the hospital. Today was a beautiful day and all Ryan could think about was having a son or daughter. A couple of hours later, it was Matt's turn to get up and put on his "corporate drag" as he referred to it, and get into work. By the time he arrived, it was nearly eight-thirty.

Before going up to the twentieth floor of his office building, Matt's morning ritual included getting his morning coffee and bagel. As he paid for his breakfast, he thought, "I have to call Mo and tell her the great news!" Getting back to his office, he arranged to have lunch with Mo, but it was very difficult not to tell her.

He knew how the conversation would go and how many questions she'd ask, "Why? What do you want to talk to me about? Why are you being so secretive? What's up now? I can't wait until lunch now that you've piqued my curiosity!"

Mo could normally smell gossip before it started. She had her ear to the ground and if there was news out there, she'd find out about it before it happened. She was great however, because she always kept the old school gang knowledgeable about what everyone else was doing and how they were.

Not knowing what Matt had to tell her was killing her however. It was about ten o'clock when Matt's phone rang.

"Are you and Ryan going to get married? I mean have a ceremony?" Mo's first words when Matt answered it.

"Actually, I hadn't thought about it, but maybe we will."

"Stop toying with me Matt! What's the news, I can't concentrate on anything else!"

"It's a good thing today's a slow business day, huh Mo?" Matt said evasively.

"Oh never mind! I'll talk to you at lunch! Goodbye." Mo hung up the phone while Matt chuckled to himself.

Around eleven o'clock Matt's phone rang again.

"You and Ryan aren't splitting up are you? I mean, that would be terrible, tell me it's not true?" Mo said anxiously.

"No, that's not it either. Don't you have anything better to do?" Matt replied.

"Of course I do, I just can't help it. Why don't you give me a hint?" said Mo.

"I know better than that. If I give you one hint, you'll either figure it out or you'll nag me into giving you another clue and then I won't get my work done," responded Matt.

"Fine. I'll meet you at the restaurant."

Matt waited for another call with another idea, worrying that she might just figure it out. Mo had a million and one ideas running around in her head and was always thinking. That's one of the reasons why she was so good at the advertising agency.

They met at a little Spanish restaurant tucked away in one of the alleys near the financial district. Mo, wearing her emerald green suit that fit her petite figure, showed up first. Obviously anxious to find out what the news was.

"Hi Matt, how are you?"

"Good, presentation today?"

"Yes. I have one at two o'clock this afternoon with my favorite client. You know, the CEO who's been around as long as dirt? I really do hate that man. He's so crotchety and never has anything good to say," Mo said bitterly, "but how did you know?"

"You always wear that suit when you have an important meeting or presentation."

Mo shrugged.

"Okay smarty pants. Now what about this news?"

"Let's order first," Matt replied, trying to tease her a little more.

"Matt Tylo, if you don't tell me this second, I'm going to explode. Now what is it?"

Matt was grinning from ear to ear.

"Ryan and I want to have a baby."

"Which one of you is going to have it?" said Mo as she laughed.

"I'm serious, Ryan and I discussed it last night and we decided that we are going to have a child. We just don't know how we are going to go about it. I'm thinking of adopting, having a surrogate mother, or maybe trying the black market."

"The black market? Tell me you're kidding, Matt?"

"Jeez, settle down! Of course I was only kidding. I'm not sure what we are going to do but it will definitely be legal."

"Have you thought about this? Really thought about this?" Mo urged.

"Of course I have. It's all I've been thinking about for the last twenty or so hours. I could barely sleep last night. You know how I've always wanted to have a baby," Matt proclaimed.

"I know, but you know how society is. People don't accept gays, gay couples, let alone gay couples with children. What people don't understand, they refuse to tolerate. It makes me sick sometimes. I can look at the relationship of any one of my straight friends, and it doesn't compare to the relationship that you and Ryan have. I can't even imagine Susan and Mark having a baby. I'm surprised they are still married, yet society would much rather see them with a baby than two people who are truly in love. I just don't understand the narrow mindedness of people," Mo preached.

"You're right. I never said it would be easy. But you know me. The only regret I've ever had about being gay is that I would never have a child. Not having my own son or daughter is just about the only thing that kills me and thinking about it is the only thing that brings tears to my eyes," Matt replied.

"Okay, don't start crying now. We haven't even ordered our lunch," Mo said laughingly.

"I won't. But you know how I feel. I'm sick of thinking about what other people will say or how they'll look at us. I don't care anymore. Why shouldn't I be happy? Who said that just because you are gay, you can't be happy or that you can't have what you truly want? I would be a great father, you know that. I'd be a better parent than Susan and Mark would be together!" Matt exclaimed.

"Of course you would. I'm on your side, remember?" Mo replied.

"Yes. That's why I feel so comfortable telling you this. So what do you think?" Matt inquired.

Mo sighed. "Adoption is supposed to be the easiest, but I don't know about with gay parents. And how do you know what kind of child you would get. I mean, the child could have the traits of a serial killer or something like that. I saw something on *60 minutes* or some news show where this family had an adopted boy and he turned out to be a criminal. He stole from them and threatened to kill them. He made their lives hell until he was finally convicted of robbery or something like that and was put in jail for a while."

"Paint a pretty picture why don't you! What about the story of a family that adopts the nicest, cutest, sweetest child that ever existed? Did you see that on *60 minutes*?"

"No, but that's not going to bring in viewers," Mo said.

"I didn't think so. Anyway, our only other option I can see is to have a surrogate mother. But I just don't know how comfortable I am about having a stranger being the mother of my child," Matt responded, not having given it too much thought.

"Yeah, she just might turn out to be the serial killer!" Mo laughed.

"Do you have anything positive to say today? What do you think I should do? Can you be serious for a minute?" Matt said.

"Did you ever think of having someone you know have the baby?" Mo asked.

"What do you mean?"

"Well, rather than have a stranger have your baby, you could ask someone you know who wants to have a baby but doesn't necessarily want a husband or even the child for that matter?"

"I don't think I know anyone like that, do you?"

"What about if I had your child?" Mo said, shocking Matt.

"You're not serious?"

"Of course I am. I told you once before that if I didn't have a husband or a child by the time I was thirty that I would consider being a surrogate mother," Mo said.

"Yes, but you know this would be too weird. You can't be serious," Matt replied.

"I don't know. I love you and Ryan and why not? I've been thinking about having a baby lately. Why? I don't know but I know that I've been paying much more attention to babies and nothing else is happening in my life right now. Maybe this is a sign of some sort?" Mo stated.

"Really? I mean, Ryan and I were thinking that we would be the baby's parents. I don't know if either one of us thought about the baby's mother being involved or around. I'm not sure it would work this way. We are too close and it might be odd for you to share your baby with us."

"Matt, you are rambling," Mo said attempting to stop Matt from over analyzing the situation.

"Of course if we did have custody of the baby, you could visit it as much as possible, but would you really want to give the child up to us?" Matt queried, thinking that Mo had not thought about this as well.

"Matt, you know I want to have a child before it's too late and you know how I feel about being a single mother. I don't know two finer people deserving of a child than you and Ryan. I'm sure I will want to play a role in the baby's life but I just don't think I would be a very good single mother. I think this is something that we could do. Who better to have as a father to my baby than my best friend?"

"We certainly don't have to decide on anything today. Let me go home, talk to Ryan and you think about it and we'll discuss it later. Right now I'm starved, let's order." Matt didn't know how he could be starving. He was so excited, nervous, and anxious all at the same time.

Two months later, Mo, Matt, and Ryan were celebrating their contract which called for Mo to have an implant of the "blended" sperm of both Matt and Ryan. It was stated that Mo would be able to see the child whenever she wanted but that Matt and Ryan were to have full custody at all times. Matt felt odd about the arrangement but they had all discussed it many times and had agreed on the terms. Mo was extremely happy. Not only would she be giving birth to a child, but she would be making a dream come true for two of her closest friends. Her only concern was not knowing how much time she would want to spend with the baby. She knew however, that Matt and Ryan would allow her as much visitation as she needed. Besides, they were very close friends and spent so much of their time together already. She couldn't imagine that changing too much. Even though they talked about how she would be more of an "aunt" to the baby, she knew in time the baby would come to know her as "mommy."

Ryan, on the other hand, wasn't sure about the arrangement but wanted a child so desperately, he'd do anything. Since that night he and Matt had seen the little boy in the restaurant, all he could do was imagine this little child coming up to him and asking him questions that only Daddy would know. After all, he had spent his career delivering babies and now it was time he had one of his own. Still, he wasn't sure about the legality of the contract so he proceeded to take it to an attorney.

The attorney stated that the contract would never hold up in a court of law. The courts still felt that a child's place is with his or her mother and "there's no court in this nation that's going to give a child to a pair of gay parents." His attorney was right. Although it was 1996, the public had come far in its acceptance of gay marriages, or commitments to which they were referred, but no one would allow a gay couple to take a child from its natural born mother.

"Oh, well," Ryan thought, "it will never come to that anyway."

CHAPTER 9

"Second Thoughts"

Two months had passed and Mo still wasn't pregnant. The doctors said that it would take some time and that it should work. He also told them that it would require patience because there were so many variables. The success rate depended on the strength, count, and mobility of the sperm, the timing, and the condition of the woman. Matt found out much more about the female body and anatomy than he ever imagined. Maureen told him how the luteinizing hormone spikes days before a woman's most fertile day of the month and how she was testing it. The doctor cautioned them that it might take up to a year before she became pregnant.

Matt began to wonder if they had done the right thing. After all, how could a mother give up her child? "I guess it's not for me to worry about, Mo knows what she's doing," he thought.

Maureen, on the other hand, found humor in the fact that maybe he and Ryan were shooting blanks and that's why she hadn't gotten pregnant.

Ryan was still hopeful and excited. He knew that it sometimes took months if not years to conceive, even without complications or problems.

It was three o'clock and just before Matt was about to make a coffee run with some of his colleagues, the phone rang.

"We're pregnant, I mean, I'm pregnant. Well, you know what I mean," gushed an exuberant Mo.

"You're kidding. When did you find out," Matt responded calmly, trying not to get too excited.

"Just now, I'm at the doctor's office and borrowed her phone. Isn't it wonderful?"

"I can't believe it, that's great. We're gonna have a baby. Now you're sure it's ours?" joked Matt.

"Matt, how could you say such a thing? I think it's yours anyway, maybe not," quipped Mo, playing along. "I have to go now. I just wanted you to be the first to know."

Matt sat down in his chair and smiled. He was going to be a father. Since the day he knew he was gay, he always felt empty thinking he would never have a child, never be a father, but now all that was changing and life was good. No, life was great.

One of his colleagues came over to where he was sitting and said, "Good news? You look like you just won the lottery?"

"Yeah, I feel like I won the lottery," Matt said evasively.

Practically everyone there knew he was gay, but he didn't think they needed to know every detail about his personal life. Not that he was ashamed of it, but he didn't think it was necessary. He always believed that, gay or straight, one's personal life didn't have a place at work. Besides, something this big wouldn't be a secret for too long. He just didn't want to tell anyone so soon, just in case there was a problem.

"Before we go I need to make a phone call, do you want to wait for me or go ahead?" Matt questioned his colleague.

"I'll wait for you; I need to finish this document anyway."

Matt then phoned Ryan, knowing that if he didn't call him at that very second, he might find out through the hospital, through Mo's doctor, or through Mo herself!

"Ryan Cavazos," the deep voice sounded on the other end of the line.

"Daddy, is that you daddy?" Matt uttered in a baby voice.

"Excuse me?" Ryan sounded bewildered.

"I'm looking for my daddy," Matt continued.

"Matt is that you?"

"Yes! How'd you know?"

"I can tell your voice, even when you try to disguise it, but really, a baby voice? Getting in touch with your childhood again, huh Matt? I can't really talk right now though, what's up?"

"Don't you get it?" Matt asked.

"Get what?" Ryan paused for a brief moment, "Are you telling me I'm…, I mean, we're going to be fathers?"

"Yep! I just found out myself," Matt responded.

"Oh wow! This calls for a celebration. Call Mo and see if she wants to go out to dinner tonight somewhere special!" Ryan sounded exuberant.

"O.k., I'll see you when we get home, bye dada!" Matt responded, again using his baby voice.

Ryan chuckled. "See you later. I love you."

※ ※ ※

For the next several months, Matt and Ryan catered to Mo, calling her at least every other day, taking her shopping for maternity clothes, treating her to dinners, and taking a half gallon of her favorite ice cream, cappuccino crunch, over to her house whenever necessary.

During her fourth month of pregnancy, she started feeling really run down and out of breath, but she figured it was just the increase in her weight.

"You know, I just don't feel the same. I feel so tired all the time and run down," she told Matt one day at lunch.

"Ryan said you'd be tired in your first semester," Matt said comfortingly.

"Trimester, Matt!" Mo laughed.

"Whatever. Semester, trimester, you know what I mean. Maybe you should consider cutting back your hours at work," Matt suggested.

"You know I could never do that. I'm needed there too badly, plus what else would I do." Mo loved working and enjoyed the rewards that came with her career. She had been promoted just before the pregnancy and didn't want it to get in the way of her career. "I don't understand why I can't have both," she said.

"You can, but maybe you just need to find the right mix. After all, you do have another life inside of you, remember." Matt was concerned about her.

"I know. I just want to have it all. You know exactly what I mean, don't you Matt?"

"Of course I do; I'm the same way, but you have to remember, you have another life to think about as well."

"Alright, I'll think about slowing down just as soon as I get this project that I'm working on done," Mo promised.

❦   ❦   ❦

It was another two months and Mo had fainted at work and had been rushed to the hospital. After several tests, they discovered that she had an unusual condition. It seemed that the blood vessels leading to her heart were very thin and the pregnancy had worsened her condition.

"How come I never knew about this sooner?" she asked her physician.

"Sometimes it's never discovered unless symptoms occur which lead us to look in that direction. We don't know if we ever would have found out," stated her doctor.

Her physician continued to tell her that she needed complete bed rest for the duration of her pregnancy. If not, she not only jeopardized the baby's health but her own. The doctor continued to tell her that her chances of surviving child birth were about seventy percent and that she should consider having a caesarean section.

"What about if I have complete bed rest?" Mo wanted more than anything to have a natural delivery.

"We'll have to judge it when the time draws nearer," said the doctor.

Matt was over at Mo's that evening. "How are you? Ryan and I are so worried about you and the baby."

"Give it a rest, Matt, you mean you're worried about the baby!" Mo blurted with a cold demeanor.

"What are you talking about? I'm just as concerned about you as I am about the baby, if not more. What's wrong with you?"

"What's wrong with me? What do you think's wrong with me? I'm sick of you and Ryan looking after me every step of the way as if you were afraid something was going to happen to *your* baby. And now, because of the baby, I'm having to pay the price!" Mo shouted.

"What? This was just as much your idea as it was ours! I don't think you should be getting upset. It's not good for you." Matt had a confused look on his face as if he didn't know who this person was he was talking to.

"Don't worry about me. I'll be fine and your precious little baby will be too!" Mo's face was different. The glow that was once evident by her pregnancy was replaced with bitterness.

"Mo, why are you acting this way?" Matt inquired with genuine concern.

"Just leave me alone Matt. Would you just go now?"

"O.K., but call me if you need anything, please."

❦   ❦   ❦

Matt was baffled by Mo's change in disposition. They had gotten along so well over the years but he knew that she had a temper and that she could change in a heartbeat. He reminisced about the time she stopped talking to him for nearly six months. She was stressing over a trigonometry final during their junior year of high school. She was complaining to Matt about not knowing the subject and how poorly she was going to do unless he helped her. Matt said that he'd help her a little bit but that he didn't have a lot of time to spend with her because he had to study for his own finals. She became very angry with him and they proceeded to get into heated conversation when Matt snapped.

"Why don't you just pay more attention in class? If you do, you wouldn't be in this situation now," he said.

"Who are you to tell me to pay more attention?" she responded.

"All I'm saying is that it's not my fault that I don't have that much time to help you," Matt countered.

"Fine. I don't need your stupid help anyway. Thanks a lot! I knew I could count on you," she said just before storming off towards her locker.

Matt was equally upset because he hadn't seen her temper before and was shaken by the confrontation. He thought at the time that she just needed time to cool off and then she'd apologize. He waited two weeks before finally calling her, only to have her mother tell him that she wasn't available even though he knew she was there. He attempted to contact her several more times before surrendering.

Matt couldn't forget that because it was the only summer that he had to figure out what to do without his best friend. When they started back at school, he ignored her. He thought that if she was going to treat him that way, then it was her problem and he didn't need to be friends with such a selfish person. Three months after they started their senior year, the high school was preparing for their homecoming festivities and they had both been nominated for king and queen. At first, Maureen was cold to Matt and attempted to avoid him. But ignored her and joked and laughed with the other candidates. Soon, Matt and Maureen found themselves chuckling at each other's funny stories and reminiscing about their past. They apologized to each other and bonded again after neither one of them were selected as the king or queen.

🍁   🍁   🍁

It had been a week and Mo wasn't taking any calls. Matt thought he'd let her stew for a while and try to talk to her the following week. Matt tried phoning her again, but no answer. Finally, he decided to visit her in person. She was now seven and a half months into her pregnancy and all checkups appeared to be fine. The doctor told Mo that she should still consider a caesarean section, but that the risk was less now that she had taken care of herself and if she still wanted to have the baby naturally, they would have monitors on her checking her vital signs should anything go wrong. This pleased her very much. The doorbell rang and the nurse who had been by her side during these last weeks answered the door.

"May I help you?"

"Yes, I'm here to see Maureen. Tell her it's Matt."

After a long wait, the door finally buzzed, and Matt made his way up the stairs to her flat and entered.

"Mo, how are you?"

"I'm fine," Mo responded, somewhat calmer than the last time they had spoken.

"Listen Mo, don't get upset or anything, but why are you acting like this?"

"You don't understand, do you Matt? Here I am in this bed, day and night, and for what, so I can hand this baby over to you and Ryan? I have sacrificed my last month and a half for you two and I'll be sacrificing the next month to month and a half for you. How would that make you feel?"

"How did any of us know that this would happen? I don't know why you are taking this out on us? We have tried to help you in every way we can and that's all you do now is turn us away. Have you forgotten that we are the best of friends? Have you forgotten everything we've gone through? Mo, you're my dearest and closest friend. You are the one I always turn to for advice or just to let off steam. Has this really changed all that?" Matt responded, teary-eyed.

"Oh Matt, I wish you wouldn't have said that. It just makes it more difficult now."

"Makes what more difficult? What are you talking about?" Matt was standing to the side of her bed with a bewildered look on his face.

Mo sat up just a bit and looked out her bedroom window. "I've decided to keep the baby. I'm sorry, I know how disappointed you are, but I have given everything up for this baby and I just can't give it away."

"Mo, you're not just giving it away. Remember Aunt Mo? You will see the child whenever you want." Matt's face turned from kindness to resentment. "Besides, you made a promise. You signed a contract. You can't do this to us. I understand you've made a sacrifice, but you're being compensated. We'll give you anything you want."

"Do you really think I'm concerned with the money? Mo said.

"Well tell me what it is that you want then," Matt pleaded.

"I want to keep my baby. That's what I want."

"You said yourself that you couldn't see yourself raising a baby on your own. What are you going to do?" Matt asked.

"I don't know. All I do know is that I can't give this baby up to you and Ryan. I can't do that after all of this."

"Mo, you promised. Won't you reconsider?" Matt posed the question.

Mo turned away from Matt and was now looking out the window, "I've thought about it for the last several days and I just can't do it. Can't you understand that?"

"Yes and no. Can't you understand our position? You proposed this to us, remember? And now you are going to take it away from us, just like that?" Matt was getting upset and could feel his heart beginning to race.

"Just like that? How can you say that? Haven't you heard a word I've said? I've been stuck in this bed for weeks. Just like that? No, I've been thinking about this for weeks. I didn't want to do this but I can't help what I feel." Mo's face was turning red from the exchange of words.

"You are being so unreasonable. Why can't we work out another arrangement? You know how much Ryan and I are desperate to have our own baby. After all, one of us is the father of that baby, don't forget that!" Matt snapped.

"Oh, I just knew you'd have to bring that up," Mo replied.

"Are you kidding me? This isn't your baby, this is our baby, whether you like it or not and we will have custody of the baby," Matt said.

"Like hell you will. Fuck you Matt. This is my baby and you know damn well that contract won't stand up in a court of law. I think you need to leave now. Nurse!" Mo summoned.

"You haven't heard the last of this yet! Not by a long shot!" Matt said just before the nurse walked into Mo's bedroom, his hands shaking with anger.

CHAPTER 10

"Circle of Life"

"Are you kidding me?" Ryan was shocked to hear Matt tell him about his encounter with Mo.

"No and she wouldn't budge on anything either," Matt said.

"How can she do this? That god-dammed bitch! After all we've done for her! I knew something like this would happen!" Ryan was furious when Matt continued to tell him the details. "That child is ours. I don't care what she says! Let me talk to her!!"

"No Ryan. It will just make matters worse. Besides, we can't jeopardize the baby's health now," Matt argued.

"Fine, but don't worry about a thing Matt. I'll see to it that we have our child!" Ryan said adamantly, "Maureen Farnsworth doesn't know who she's dealing with."

It was the first time Matt had seen Ryan so upset. It, in fact, scared him. The expression on Ryan's face showed hatred and revulsion. It was as if Matt was now looking at someone completely different and he didn't like it. He wanted to say something but had no idea what to say. He was spooked by Ryan's behavior.

He sighed and thought, "How did we ever get into this situation?"

Matt tried to reason with Mo, but it was futile. Each time they talked the conversation ended with an argument until one day Mo's nurse put a halt to it.

"Matt, I'm sorry but Maureen's very close to delivery and she really needs her rest now and she can't afford to be upset. You understand," the nurse told him.

Matt didn't know what to say so he just hung up the phone.

Despite Matt's pleading with him, Ryan thought he would call her to see if he could reason with her. The only reason he got through was because the nurse didn't recognize his voice.

"Mo, please change your mind. You know we have a contract and that this can all work out for all of us."

"I've already told Matt what you guys can do with your contract, so why don't you take turns with it?" Mo said irately.

Ryan took a deep breath so he wouldn't get any angrier, "I understand what you are going through, I really do. You have to know that Matt and I want to work out what is best for all of us and I think you are being selfish.

"You mean you want it all to work out for you and Matt! What about me? You're nothing but a selfish bastard!" Mo bellowed.

"I was hoping we could have a civilized conversation. Maybe we can talk about this after you have the baby. Your hormones won't be raging as much then and I'm sure you'll be thinking differently," Ryan suggested.

"Don't patronize me and don't give me your doctor spiel about hormones as if you know what you are talking about anyway! Just leave me the fuck alone! Don't you guys get it? YOU ARE NOT GETTING THIS BABY. It is mine and I am not giving him or her up to anyone. I'm sorry but that's just it. Go find someone else," Maureen shouted.

"You good for nothing bitch! If you weren't so fucking cold, you could probably have your own man and child, but no-you have to rely on a gay man to have a child. You're pathetic!" Ryan was outraged.

"How dare you!" Mo responded.

"Just wait. We'll have that baby. I guarantee it. If it's the last thing I do, I'm going to see to it that Matt and I have our just-deserved child!"

Mo threw down the phone.

The stress had taken its toll on everyone. Matt's performance at work was declining and he was waking up during the middle of the night-unable to go back to sleep. He was worried about Ryan and was shocked to see how he had changed over the last month. Ryan seemed to be a different person and was so full of anger. Matt was no longer running or exercising. "What's the point?" he'd say without any visible energy.

Ryan couldn't remember the last time they'd made love and he was concerned about Matt's health. He'd lost ten pounds and looked sickly.

"Matt, you've got to stop worrying about this. It will all work out, somehow!"

"How Ryan? How do you think it's all going to work out?" Matt inquired.

"I don't know, but it just has to. Maybe after she has the baby she'll start thinking clearly and come to her senses. I promise. You have to be positive about the whole thing. We'll have a baby. I'm going to see to it that this works out for all of us, okay?" Ryan said comfortingly.

Matt's face brightened. "Okay. You're the boss."

※ ※ ※

It was a Thursday night. The fog had rolled in and it was getting cold and damp. Ryan had gone back to the hospital to complete an article he was writing for one of the medical journals. He had been at the hospital for six hours already trying to finish it but was disrupted twice because of emergencies. There were several doctors out and for some reason, maybe because of the full moon, there were a lot of visitors in the E.R. that night. He finished and was on his way out when on of the nurse's approached him.

"Doctor Cavazos, we need your help," she pleaded.

"Not again, are you kidding me? Ryan questioned.

"I'm sorry sir but you know how short staffed we are tonight."

"What's the emergency this time?" he asked.

"A pregnant woman was just brought in and the doctor on call is busy with another emergency."

"Isn't there anyone else who can help?" Ryan asked.

"All of our E.R. docs are busy with the patients from the hotel fire," replied the nurse.

"Hotel fire? What hotel?" Ryan replied.

"I'm not sure but there was a huge fire and we've had to set up triage in the emergency room because we are expecting close to a hundred more patients tonight," the nurse answered.

"Alright," Ryan said calmly, "page her doctor and I'll have a look at her."

"We've been paging her doctor, but she hasn't responded."

Ryan and the nurse took the three flights of stairs down to the emergency room. Ryan nearly collapsed when he walked in and saw the patient. It was Mo.

"Where's my doctor?" She pleaded and then turned to see Ryan, "Ryan, help me. Help me deliver my baby, please!" Mo screamed hysterically.

Ryan froze for a minute, took a deep breath and said, "Everything's going to be alright. Just calm down and I'll be right back."

"Doctor, where are you going?" the nurse was flabbergasted that he was walking out.

Ryan took the nurse aside, "I have to wash and prepare for delivery. She's going to have this baby now. Get her prepped."

"Yes doctor."

Ryan returned to the emergency room. "Here's something to put you at ease."

"Will it harm the baby?" Mo asked. Even though she was in pain, her first concern was still the baby.

"Not at all. Don't worry about a thing," reassured Ryan as he examined her and reviewed her chart. "Let's prep her for delivery."

"There aren't any rooms available, doctor," the nurse responded.

"Don't tell me there aren't any rooms available. We need a room and we need one now," Ryan demanded.

"What about curtain three? Will that do?" She asked.

"No! It has to be a private room. Move someone out so we can get her into one, NOW!" he said.

"Yes, doctor."

Maureen let out a scream, "Is everything going to be okay?"

"It will be fine. Don't worry about it. Take deep breaths in between your contractions," said Ryan.

"We can move into Room Four," the nurse said, as she reentered into the room.

"Okay, let's go," Ryan said.

The nurse wheeled her away. It was 7:42 pm. "How are her vitals?" Ryan asked.

The nurse responded, "Her heart rate seems to be dropping. I'm not sure why."

Normally a woman's blood pressure rose during delivery so this stumped the nurse.

"Is something wrong?" Mo asked in between her contractions.

"I told you not to worry. I've got everything under control Maureen," he said.

Maureen had been in there for a half an hour, pushing with each contraction and was tired. Her face was pale and she was wet with sweat. The nurse asked her several times if there was anything she could do for her but Maureen was stubborn and wanted the delivery to be over.

"How much longer?" she asked.

"I'm not sure, just keep pushing. You are doing fine."

"I feel light-headed and I can't catch my breath," Mo said.

"Should I give her some oxygen, doctor?" asked the nurse.

"Yes," Ryan said and looked up at Mo, "come on now, you are going to have dig down and really push if you want this to be over."

"I'm trying," Mo responded.

"Well, you are going to have to try a little harder. Come on now, you are almost there," he said.

"Doctor, her blood pressure is one-hundred over sixty now," stated the nurse, "should we give her something?"

"The only thing she needs now is to have this baby. It's too late to give her anything. It might jeopardize the delivery," Ryan said.

The nurse turned up the oxygen and Mo continued to push for another ten minutes.

"O.K. Maureen, are you ready? I'm going to have you push as hard as you can. Let's do it."

"Wait. I'm sorry Ryan. I'm sorry for everything that's happened," pleaded Mo as tears rolled down her face.

The nurse looked puzzled. Ryan noticed her reaction and shrugged his shoulders.

"Don't worry about any of that now. Let's just deliver a healthy and beautiful baby," Ryan said.

"Alright." Mo started pushing. She was becoming more light-headed and now she was feeling cold. She didn't have an ounce of energy left inside her.

"I can see the head, come on Maureen, just a couple more pushes and were done," encouraged Ryan.

"You can do it honey," said the nurse.

Mo pushed one more time and Ryan was able to reach the baby and with a pull on its shoulders was able to deliver it.

All attention was on the baby. "It's a girl," one of the nurses screamed with enthusiasm.

It was 8:33 pm and Jacqueline Marie was born. The pediatric nurse took Jacqueline and began working on her in the corner of the room. They began sucking the mucus out of her nostrils and mouth to make sure her air passages were clean and clear. They applied the APGAR test to measure the baby's heart rate, respiration, muscle tone, reflex responsiveness, and skin color.

Ryan turned to the team working on the baby and said, "How is she?"

"She's beautiful and healthy," the nurse said with a big grin on her face.

The nurse turned to Mo and told her that she had a beautiful little girl but she was still. The nurse shook her but could see that there wasn't any breathe in her.

"Doctor, we have a problem," she immediately removed the oxygen mask from Maureen's face, reclined her bed to a full horizontal position, and began checking her for a pulse. "She's not responding Doctor," the nurse said.

"Maureen, Maureen!" yelled Ryan who then turned to the pediatric team, "Get that baby up to the nursery to finish your tests."

The nurse was slapping Maureen's face to awaken her, but there was no reaction. The nurse looked at her vitals.

At the same time Ryan glimpsed at the monitors and yelled, "She's flat lining." It was all happening so fast.

"We have a code blue," the nurse said.

"Get that equipment over here," Ryan hollered, "clear the way so I can work on her!"

"We need to bag her," Ryan said to the nurse, "get me the supplies while I work on chest compressions?"

The next thirty minutes were the most frantic as Ryan tried to resuscitate her. It was difficult to work on someone you knew. All the doctors told him that during his first year at the hospital but up until that night, he had only imagined what it would feel like. He now knew how difficult it was as he was feeling an array of emotions. He felt fear, compassion, anxiety, remorse, sadness, and isolation. He recalled the hatred in Mo's voice the last time they spoke and how disgusted she looked the last time he saw her. It was a time when she was also filled with many emotions. As he looked back at her, laying there on the table, she was now pale and calm. He knew she would have to be operated on because she was losing a lot of blood.

"Get a surgeon in here now," he yelled at one of the other nurses who had just entered upon hearing the code blue distress.

The nurse looked at him in bewilderment, "Who should I get?"

"How the hell should I know?" Ryan looked at the nurse who had been helping him, "Who's on staff?" He didn't wait for her response, "Just get someone who can operate on her A.S.A.P. We are losing her. She's bleeding internally."

Ryan knew there was nothing that he could do for her. He might attempt to open her up, find the place from where she was bleeding but he hadn't done that in a long while and knew it was against hospital regulations. If anything were to go wrong or if she were to die, the hospital would be liable. He continued with the chest compressions.

"Wheel that crash cart over here," he beckoned.

He applied the paddles to her chest, "Charge to one-hundred. Clear," he yelled with sweat rolling down his forehead and into his eyes. He was getting more and more upset. It had been forty five minutes since she was down and knew they didn't have much more time.

"Where's the doctor? Charge to one-forty! Clear."

"Nothing doctor," the nurse said as she continued to use the bag to supply oxygen to Mo.

"Charge to two-hundred," he said in a last attempt to revive her. He debated on whether he should open her chest and repair whatever damage awaited him but knew he would only be making matters worse. The proper equipment wasn't readily available and he hadn't performed an operation, other than a caesarian in more than a year. He finally worked up enough courage to tell the nurse, "Get me a scalpel!"

"Doctor, shouldn't you wait for a surgeon?" she said.

"There's no time," Ryan said before one of the emergency room doctors entered the room.

"What do we have here," he said.

Ryan quickly stated the facts and stepped back so that the surgeon could work on Mo.

"How long has she been down?" he said.

Ryan hesitated so the nurse responded, "it's been about forty-five minutes."

Ryan moved to the other side of the bed to assist the doctor. The nurse was frantically trying to get supplies she knew they would need. Ryan took a look at Mo's face while the doctor opened her chest. He was doing everything in his power to hold back his emotions. His heart was racing. He wanted this night to start over. He thought about his decisions and wondered if he had done the right thing.

During his rotation at the hospital one of his mentors had told him, "You don't know how good of a doctor you are until you are in the midst of an emergency because that is when your instincts take over and that is when you will either succeed or fail."

It was now 9:47pm and the surgeon officially pronounced Maureen Marie Farnsworth dead.

He looked around the room to see the sorrow on the faces of Ryan and the two nurses.

"We did all we could do," the surgeon said, trying to lift their spirits.

Ryan stood there for a minute, looking at the bloody mess that lay before him. He took a step back as a tear fell from his face.

"There wasn't anything you could have done, doctor," said the surgeon, "Two of her major arteries erupted because of the strain, I'm sure. Even if I had made it in here a half an hour ago, I'm not sure I would have been able to save her. You were lucky to have delivered the baby."

Ryan felt sick to his stomach and walked out of the emergency room. He rushed to the bathroom where he proceeded to splash water on his face. What had just happened? He held onto the basin of the sink so tightly that his knuckles were white.

"Oh God, how am I going to tell Matt?" he pleaded for help and the courage to get through this.

"I need you to come down to the hospital right now," was the only thing Matt remembered hearing when Ryan called. Ryan wouldn't give him any details and as he was rushing to the hospital, he was trying to prepare himself for whatever situation presented itself.

As Matt walked down the corridor, he saw Ryan slumped over in a chair. His breathing was becoming more rapid the closer he got. He stood in front of him and Ryan looked up at him. His eyes were red.

"Just tell me what it is Ryan," Matt was shaking in anticipation and fear, "is it the baby? Is it Mo?"

"It's Mo," was all Ryan could say.

"Were there complications? How is she?" Matt asked cautiously.

"Matt, sit down," Ryan asked calmly.

"No, no! I'm not sitting down," the tears fell from Matt's eyes, "just tell me what it is. Tell me she's okay."

"I can't Matt. She's dead," Ryan replied.

"Oh, God! No! No!" Matt fell to his knees.

Ryan leaned over and picked him up and hugged him.

"Here, sit down."

"I can't believe it. Tell me it's not true! Tell me! Tell me!" Matt pleaded.

"I wish I could, but I can't."

"This can't be happening. I think I'm going to be sick."

Ryan fought for something to say but couldn't think of anything that would comfort the love of his life.

"I don't believe this. I don't believe it. Ryan, please tell me…"

"I can't believe it myself Matt but it's true," Ryan told him.

Matt sobbed for several more minutes.

"I was all she had. Can I see her?" Matt asked

"I don't think that would be a good idea. The surgeon had to open her up to see if he could save her and there's quite a mess," Ryan said.

"What happened? How's the baby?" Matt questioned.

"The baby's fine. She's up in the nursery right now," Ryan replied.

"She? Mo had a girl?" Matt said as tears fell again from his face, "I knew she wanted a girl. I'm sure she looks just like her."

Although he kept out the gory details of what happened, Ryan told Matt how Mo's heart just gave out because of the stress from the delivery.

"We killed her Ryan. This is our fault."

"Don't be ridiculous Matt. This is not our fault. Maureen knew the risks associated with her illness. She knew that a natural childbirth was dangerous and it was her decision, don't forget that," Ryan said trying to console him.

"But if we hadn't agreed to this whole dim-witted idea of having a baby, none of this would have happened. We wouldn't have been at each others throats and she'd be alive today," Matt said.

"How can you say that? You've always wanted a baby. Matt, she agreed to it, too. She wanted the baby just as much as we did. Don't lose sight on the fact that she was going to keep our baby, remember?"

"I don't want to talk about it," Matt responded emotionless.

"Do you want to see the baby now?" inquired Ryan.

"In a minute. I need to see Mo. Can you let me know when I can see her?" requested Matt.

"I'll go and find out. Will you be okay?" Ryan asked.

"Yes. I'm fine." Matt was numb and composed. His face was cold.

Ryan wasn't sure what to say except, "I'm sorry Matt."

He was indeed sorry. He was sorry it had to come to this, but Ryan knew he had to seize the opportunity when he saw it. And when he saw Mo lying on the gurney in the emergency room, he realized this was his chance. The idea had come to him so naturally, it scared him. When he dismissed himself from the emergency room to clean up, he ran to the room that held their medications. His hand was shaking as he grabbled for the key from his key ring. He knew he didn't have a lot of time and he had to get in and out of there as fast as possible. He quickly scanned the shelves to find what he was looking for and there it was on the second shelf. He snatched the vile of Hydralazine which he would administer to Mo. He knew that with her condition, it would be lethal. During the stress of delivery, her heart rhythm and blood vessels would be racing. The drug would relax and dilate her blood vessels which would tax her heart even more. With any luck, he hoped that the strain of delivery would cause her ventricles to burst. Any doctor knowing her condition wouldn't suspect a thing and no one would think to look for any drugs. It worked just as he planned.

He knew that when the drug invaded her blood stream, there would be nothing they could do for her. During the ordeal, he debated whether he had done the right thing. It wasn't until after she died that Ryan thought about Matt. He knew the news would be devastating to him but that was a small price to pay for their very own baby.

Matt was indeed devastated. He couldn't even see the baby. She reminded him too much of Maureen and now that she was gone, his whole world collapsed. When it came time to bring the baby home, Matt was no help.

"You get her and bring her home," he said, "I can't do it."

After Ryan phoned Matt's mother, she came to visit them and to help take care of Jacqueline Marie. She tried to get through to Matt. She tried getting him to talk about his emotions or the baby but he wouldn't. Ryan tried getting him to see a grief counselor but Matt refused. Matt's only focus was on the funeral arrangements. The news of her death was all over the paper. "Tragedy", "despair", "heartbreak", "anguish" were words that were plastered all throughout the articles and the news. It was horrible the way the press was making such a big deal out of her death. The newscasters sensationalized the story, focusing on the horror of a mother losing her life during delivery. When the media found out that the baby was going to be raised by two gay fathers, the story took on another life. Ryan and Matt couldn't get any rest with all the requests for interviews. Even the big news magazines wanted to interview them but they refused. Matt was becoming more withdrawn and wouldn't speak about the topic at all. People offered him their condolences but he didn't hear them. He was tired of hearing about it and wanted nothing more to do with the news or the television. At home, he sat in his bedroom, staring out the window. He could see the sun shining but it was hollow. His life wasn't real anymore. He had already experienced too many deaths but this was the worst.

He and Maureen knew each other so well; they finished each other's sentences. Each of them knew that the other loved them no matter what. "Why did our lives have to end this way," he thought. "Why did she have to die with us at each other's throats? We only wanted fulfilling lives. Did we ask for too much? Did we do something wrong and this was our payback?" Matt had plenty of questions but no answers. He should have never pushed the pregnancy or the custody of the baby. For that, he was remorseful. Time seemed to stand still for him. He tried to reach out and find something positive but couldn't. With everyone else who had died, he was always able to find relief and comfort. He couldn't see how this made any sense and wished he had died instead. He thought about that for a long time. If he had died, there would be no need for Ryan to have the baby. He was sure that Ryan wouldn't want to raise a child without him.

He imagined Maureen sitting in the nursery they had prepared for the baby before their argument. The sun shined brightly through the window and cascaded across her face. He could smell the baby lotion. He saw Mo sitting in the rocking chair, cooing at the baby, smiling. She looked up at him and her face changed. She was no longer smiling. Her face was tranquil, void of any sentiment. She became very white. As she sat there staring at him a tear fell down her cheek. As he looked closer at her, the tear had become blood and represented the only color in his vision. The crimson tear fell from her cheek onto her lap. The baby was now gone and Mo began to fade away.

"It should have been me," Matt thought over and over, "I wish it had been me."

CHAPTER 11

"The Thief"

The sun was shining brightly. The suntan lotion Ryan put on Matt was absorbing the sun's heat. Matt smelled the ripened pineapple and sweet sensation of the strawberries sitting on the table beside him. Ryan was in the ocean swimming. Maureen reached over to grab a strawberry.

"Why don't you join him?" she said.

"I will in a minute. I'm happy right here for now," he said smiling, "What are you trying to do, get rid of me?"

"No. I just thought you might want to be with Ryan, that's all," Mo responded.

"How's your margarita? I think this one is stronger than my last one," Matt said.

"It's great. I can't remember a time when I've been so relaxed and have had so much fun," Mo replied, "I'm so glad we planned this getaway. It's been a long time coming! Do you think I'm getting too much sun?"

"No, you look great," Matt said, noticing that she had a great tan and was very dark. The darkest he'd ever seen her. He looked at himself and noticed that he, too had a great tan.

They sat there laughing and listening to the ocean's waves crash onto the beach where they were laying. Matt started to fall asleep. The rum and sun were taking their effect on him. He heard the birds chirping in the palm tree far above his head.

"Grab the frisbee Matt," Mo said, startling him.

"What?"

"Grab the frisbee and let's play in the ocean with Ryan."

Matt looked around for the frisbee, realizing he had been using it as a headrest while he snoozed. As he turned back to look at Mo, she was already in the ocean, waving to him.

"Come on in. The water is awesome!" she said.

They tossed the frisbee back and forth for a long time and then Matt realized that Ryan wasn't anywhere around.

"Where's Ryan," he asked Mo.

"He's over there," Mo was pointing further out into the ocean. Ryan was floating with his face buried in the water.

"Oh my God!" Matt yelled.

Ryan looked up, "What are you yelling about?"

"Dammit Ryan, that's not funny!"

Ryan and Mo were laughing hysterically.

"You're too serious Matt," Ryan argued.

Matt moved to the lounge chairs that had been nicely placed under a palm tree to provide them with some shade from the sun. Ryan was to his right and Mo was to his left.

"Isn't it wonderful, Matt?" Mo asked.

"It's okay," he replied as they laughed, "I think I'm in heaven."

"I know I am," Mo said but she wasn't laughing and had a somber look on her face.

Matt was puzzled by her expression and was about to ask her what the problem was when he heard a loud noise. It sounded like bells ringing. Was the noise coming from the church in town? Surely he couldn't hear them all the way out at the resort where they were staying.

"Do you hear that?" he asked.

"Hear what?" Mo replied.

Matt couldn't figure out where the noise was coming from but it was annoying him. "What is that?" he asked himself.

He opened his eyes and realized it was his alarm and he had been dreaming.

"Dammit!" he thought, "We were having so much fun."

For a moment, he could feel her again, sense her spirit, and laugh with her again. The reality of Mo's death came rushing back to him. He started to grieve all over again.

The funeral was difficult for Matt. As much as he and Mo argued during the last months of the pregnancy, they had been friends for more than twenty years. She was his best friend and understood him better than anyone, including Ryan. Ryan had been very comforting during the last couple of weeks, but something was wrong. He seemed preoccupied and was reacting differently than someone who had lost a friend or a patient. He had been so strong and courageous over the last weeks that it seemed odd for him to be behaving this way now. Matt thought it was probably because Ryan had been there the night Mo went into the hospital and was blaming himself for her death. Matt told Ryan several times that he couldn't blame himself, that he was good doctor, and that there was nothing he could have done to save her life. Ryan didn't seem to respond to Matt's attempts to console him and Maureen's death didn't seem to be the problem but Matt couldn't figure it out. He decided to question him.

"What's wrong Ryan? You've been acting really weird lately."

"She died in my care, Matt. That tends to have an effect on you!" Ryan snapped.

Questions had been raised at the hospital with Maureen's death. However, Ryan had been able to answer them all and avoided investigation. He was thankful of that, especially after the hospital administration found out that Matt and Ryan had custody of the baby. The hospital administrator called him into his office privately and asked him, "Is there anything you want to tell me, off the record?"

"No. What would I have to say that I haven't already told everyone else?" Ryan answered.

"Dr. Cavazos, you have to know this is going to look a little odd and suspicious to some people," the administrator continued.

"Maybe to someone who had reason for suspicion but I have gone over and over the events of that night with the administration here, the review board, and in my own mind. There's nothing I could have done. I am at least sure of that," Ryan professed.

"Alright. I have to tell you though that there may be further investigation into the matter, simply because you and your lover are now the sole parents of the child," warned the Administrator.

"I understand that and I have nothing to hide like I've said from the very beginning," Ryan said.

Matt decided to leave Ryan alone and let him deal with his feelings, especially since he couldn't relate to what a doctor must go through when they lose a patient.

Still, Ryan's behavior was taking a toll on their relationship and Matt needed to talk to someone about it. He needed to talk to someone who wasn't involved in the whole mess, so he called his friend Cassie. Matt discussed how he and Ryan had not been getting along and how he had been so distraught over Mo's death but just then was coming to terms with everything that had happened. He told her that Ryan had slowly been retreating into his own depression.

"Matt, there's something fishy there," Cassie urged, speaking of Ryan's behavior.

"The last time I was over for dinner, I definitely thought something was wrong, but I didn't want to say anything. I figured if there was something going on between you two, you would eventually say something."

"What are you talking about?" Matt replied, "I'm sure it's just stress at work."

"It's more than that. I can tell and you know what they say about a woman's intuition," Cassie said.

"I also know how many times you've been wrong, Miss Intuition." Matt laughed.

"Matt, I'm serious!" Cassie said solemnly, "There's something weird about the way Ryan's been behaving. Have you ever talked to him about what happened the night Mo had Jacqueline Marie?"

Matt was surprised with her alarming comment and responded, "Yes. We talked about it briefly but it was too upsetting for him to talk about. I think he blames himself."

"Why would he if he didn't do anything wrong," Cassie said.

"What are you saying? Do you have any idea what a doctor goes through when he loses a patient?" Matt said firmly.

"I don't know Matt. The whole thing was a little too convenient, don't you think?"

"For God's sake Cassie, are you telling me you think Ryan had something to do with Mo's death? You watch entirely too much T.V."

"I'm not sure what I'm saying. Maybe he didn't try to save her as well as he could have," Cassie suggested.

"Will you think about what you are saying?" Matt argued, "There were nurses all around him, the same nurses that stood up for him when the hospital investigated the situation. It was Mo's condition. It was one of those things. No one could have done anything for her at that point. Now I don't want to discuss this ever again!"

"Okay. I'm sorry," Cassie responded, "I was just trying to figure out why he's been acting the way he has. I was just speculating Matt, alright? You said yourself that something seemed wrong. I won't mention it again."

A month had passed since the funeral and Matt had been very quiet and hadn't been excited about Jacqueline Marie. He hadn't mentioned anything about Mo's death because he didn't want to further upset Ryan but he couldn't hold his emotions in any longer.

"Every time I see her, I see Mo," Matt said as tears rolled down his face, "I knew she was going to have a difficult time with the delivery, but in my worst nightmares, I never ever thought it would turn out this way."

Ryan tried to be sympathetic, but had had enough of the mourning and the distance that was growing between him and Matt. Searching for something that would snap Matt out of his depression, Ryan responded by saying, "Matt, you have to get over this. What happened happened. We can't change the past. You have a daughter now. We have a family. You don't have to forget about Maureen, but think about our family. Think about our new life!"

"I know. You're right. I just need some time," Matt replied.

Ryan's composure seemed to change at that moment. Matt could tell something was brewing inside of Ryan. Ryan's face became flushed and the expression of solace changed to one of anger.

Ryan quipped, "Why do we have to go through this? What the hell did we ever do to deserve this? All we wanted was to have a child to share our love. Was that too much to ask for!?

Matt, taken aback by Ryan's actions, timidly replied, "Not at all but it's over now, Ryan, why are you so angry?

"I'm just tired of the whole thing. The way it's affected you and how it's affecting me. When will this end?"

Matt, trying to understand exactly what Ryan meant asked, "You're not still having problems with the hospital are you?"

"No, not anymore," Ryan retorted.

After taking a deep breathe and appearing to come to his senses, he said, "I'm sorry. It's nothing I can't handle anyway. I'll be fine. We'll be fine."

To help them put the past behind them, Ryan arranged a little vacation for Matt, Jacqueline, and himself to the Outer Banks of North Carolina for some rest and relaxation. Ryan knew that the ocean and beach always provided Matt with comfort and positive energy that he couldn't get elsewhere. Ryan had never been there but always wanted to go and thought it would be the perfect remedy for them both.

In just a couple of weeks, Matt was acting like his usual self and had a renewed zest for life.

Several months after their trip, Ryan was restless again. He was coming home later each night, and when he did manage to make it home at a reasonable hour for dinner, Matt noticed that he wouldn't eat much. Not only was his appetite diminishing but Ryan was getting less and less sleep. He was letting his appearance go as well. Matt was hesitant to bring up the conversation because Ryan had been so short-tempered but he did anyway.

"Ryan, what's wrong with you? I'm concerned."

"There's nothing wrong with me. What's wrong with you? Can't you see I'm overworked?" Ryan snapped.

"Okay, there's no need to bite my head off! I'm just concerned," Matt replied with sharpness.

"I'm sorry. I guess I'm a little more run down than I thought," Ryan responded unconvincingly.

Matt knew there was more to Ryan's mood than just exhaustion from the hospital but had no idea what it was.

Searching for something to say, Matt finally said, "I don't care what the matter is. I just want us to get back to some form of normalcy."

With a look of bewilderment and disgust on his face, Ryan exploded, "How do you define normal? What is it? To get back to normalcy implies that we were there once before. Were we? What do you consider normal?"

Worried about the direction of the conversation, Matt muttered, "I don't know myself. I guess I just wish things were the way we had planned them."

Ryan's appearance suddenly changed and he now had a crazed look in his eyes, "Don't worry. Everything will be exactly the way we planned it, real soon!"

"What do you mean by that?" Matt questioned.

Ryan appeared to be even more disturbed yet calm.

"I just mean that I'm gonna take care of everything that's bothering me so we can have the life we deserve and fought so hard for."

Matt had no idea to what Ryan was referring and debated whether to ask him what he meant but knew that Ryan would probably get even more upset. Instead, he simply responded with, "That's all I want, too, you know."

Matt tried to appear as though everything was fine but couldn't help sense that there was still something bothering Ryan, something that he couldn't explain. Something that maybe he didn't want to know.

Matt and Ryan had always been able to communicate. It was what Matt always said was the foundation of a relationship. If a couple couldn't communicate, they were doomed because each person would never be able to understand the other's position and would always have to second guess what the other was thinking, feeling, or doing. One of the things Matt loved and what he found to be so refreshing when he met Ryan was his ability to express himself and willingness to discuss their feelings and what they wanted out of their lives. It seemed as if their conversations were always the same now—Matt didn't know any more at the conclusion of their conversation than when they started.

🍁　　🍁　　🍁

It was now June and the weather was warming. Matt was the first to awaken and heard a bird chirping outside their bedroom window. He could smell the crisp coolness of the morning air. He turned over and saw Ryan's face and noticed how innocent and calm he looked. He looked different than he had over the last several months. He was clean shaven and was taking focused on his appearance as he had been in the past. He seemed to be sleeping comfortably and seemed content once again. Matt felt the same attraction as he did the day they first met. He leaned toward him and kissed him on the cheek and placed his arm over his chest and cuddled.

Ryan awakened. "Good morning, sweetheart."

He then turned to look out the window and said, "What a glorious morning. I bet you it's going to be a beautiful day. Hell, it might even be warm. How about if I take the day off and we go to the park. I only have a couple of appointments and I'm sure I can re-schedule them."

"Are you sure?" Matt said excitedly.

Matt didn't know what had changed but Ryan sounded like his old self again and Matt wasn't going to question it.

"Of course I am. I feel like I have a renewal on life. Let's go," Ryan responded.

Matt agreed and after breakfast, they got Jacqueline dressed and headed to Golden Gate Park where they played frisbee, basked in the sun, and ate a picnic lunch that Ryan had prepared. Matt felt like he was in heaven. Their lives had taken such a turn after Mo's death and finally, it seemed to be coming together again. It was the first time in months that he really believed they would be alright. He didn't know what exactly had changed, nor did he care. It was the first romantic moment in nearly a year.

Toward the end of the day, Ryan asked Matt if he wanted to go for a walk over the Golden Gate Bridge at sunset.

Although Matt thought it would be wonderfully romantic, he said, "I think that's a great idea, but Jacqueline's tired and I think we should head home."

"You're right," Ryan agreed, "I don't know what's come over me but I feel terrific."

A week later, Matt picked up the paper and noticed that a nurse, Kathy Davis, from the same hospital Ryan worked was slain in her apartment. Matt, holding the paper, went into their bedroom and interrupted Ryan as he was getting dressed for the day.

"Did you know Kathy Davis?" Matt inquired.

"What? Yeah, why? What do you mean did I know her?" Ryan answered.

"She was murdered last night in her apartment. They think it happened as a result of a burglary."

Ryan sat on the bed with a puzzled look on his face.

"Oh my God. Let me see it."

Ryan read the article intensely and mumbled, "Wow. I can't believe it. She was so kind, too. I really enjoyed working with her. She was a great nurse. What makes someone do such a thing?"

Matt, searching for something to console Ryan, responded, "I don't know dear. Are you going to be alright?"

The article stated that Kathy Davis, forty-two, had been stabbed at least fifteen times and that her throat had been slashed. Although they thought it was an apparent robbery, detectives could not determine whether anything had been taken. The article went on to say that there had been items tossed around in the living room area and in the kitchen but that she had been murdered while she slept in her bedroom situated down a long hallway. Detectives were following up on other possibilities. As Matt read the article he thought it was odd that she was murdered in her bedroom. If the person or persons were there to rob her, why kill her, especially if she was in her bedroom all the way down the hallway. If she was in bed asleep, she obviously didn't hear them or interrupt them. So why kill her? Something didn't seem right about the whole story, but then again, Matt knew that only half the truth was ever printed and that he would never be able to figure it out based on what he read. Perhaps they were searching the house, went into her bedroom and she awoke. She would have been able to identify them so maybe that's why they killed her. Whatever happened, he didn't want to think about it anymore.

CHAPTER 12

"Discovery"

"Matt, did you read the paper today?" asked Cassie with hesitation in her voice.

"Yes, why?" Matt replied.

"Kathy Davis, a nurse from Ryan's hospital was murdered!" she exclaimed.

"I know. What about it?"

"Don't you think that's weird?"

"That someone was murdered? No. It happens all the time. What's so weird about that?" Matt said.

"I mean that she worked with Ryan and now she's dead!" Cassie responded.

"Oh, don't start this again!"

"Come on Matt, don't you think that's a little strange?"

"No. It's just a fluke, a coincidence. People die all the time. What does it matter that she worked with Ryan? What are you going to say when someone from my firm dies?" Matt asked abruptly. He was upset that she was again bringing this topic up.

"Would it surprise you to know that she was one of the nurses who was with Mo the night she went into labor and delivered the baby?" Cassie inquired.

"How do you know that?"

"Her name sounded familiar for some reason so I went back to the article in the paper that covered the story about Maureen's death. It stated that one of the nurses, Kathy Davis, had refused to comment. I think her name stuck with me because I thought it was odd at the time," Cassie recalled.

- 106 -

"Why? Because she didn't comment? Most of the time hospital staff can't say anything to the press until the internal investigation is complete anyway," Matt informed her.

"Yes, but she didn't have any comments even after the internal investigation," she countered.

"Maybe she didn't comment to the press, but she supported Ryan. All of the nurses did. I think you are letting you're imagination run wild. Haven't you anything better to do?" Matt asked.

"Well, actually I don't." she quipped. "I still think it's too much of a coincidence."

"They said it was a robbery, Cassie, didn't you read the article?" Matt questioned.

"Yes, but didn't you think it was a little odd that she was murdered in bed," Cassie asked, "I mean the way she was murdered. Why did they have to slash her throat and stab her so many times? It just doesn't make sense to me. It doesn't seem like a robbery gone bad, if you ask me."

"I didn't ask you! Listen Agatha Christie, you figure it out. And when you do, why don't you go to the police and tell them your theory? I'm sure they'd appreciate the help!" Matt said humoring her.

"Why can't you just consider the possibility?" Cassie said.

"If you ask me, I think they started off robbing her and then decided to take a look around the apartment, found her in the bed and killed her. Do you really think you know more than the police? For crying out loud, Cassie, give it a rest!" Although Matt also thought it was odd, he had reached this conclusion and tried to convince himself as much as he did Cassie.

"Fine," Cassie said, although Matt didn't think that this was the last he would hear of it.

Certainly Ryan couldn't have anything to do with it. Not his Ryan. Not the man he knew and loved. Ryan wouldn't be a part of anything like that. Besides, he was incapable of murder! Why would he be involved? How could he benefit from her murder anyway? For God's sake, he was a doctor committed to saving lives and bringing new lives into this world. He couldn't be involved in anything like murder. Matt thought about how upset Ryan had been, but he was better now and that was all that mattered.

Three months later the only thing on Matt's mind was what he was going to do to celebrate his daughter's first birthday. What was he going to do for her birthday? Maybe Ryan would have an idea.

When Ryan came home that night, he and Matt discussed their different options and finally decided on a small gathering with special friends and family. After all, it was also the one year anniversary of Mo's death so they didn't think it was appropriate to have a huge party. Jacqueline Marie wouldn't know the difference anyway.

The invitations were sent, the calls were made, and the scene was set. Matt figured out what food he'd served and what his and Ryan's daughter was going to wear that day. Her birthday fell on a Saturday, so it was perfect for an afternoon luncheon. During the birthday party, Jacqueline Marie was an angel. She laughed and played with her new toys. Toward the end of the party, Matt remembered a gift that he had purchased several months before and had placed on the top shelf of their shelf in his and Ryan's closet. He laughed at the idea of putting her gift on the top of shelf. It wasn't like she was going to look for her gift, let alone on top of the shelf. She was only a year old and was more concerned about trying to walk than anything else. Matt stretched his arms out to reach the present. He couldn't quite grab it and had to push and prod at it to get it down. As the present got closer, a small envelope dropped from the shelf. He made a final attempt at the present and was able to pull it down. He sat it on the floor next to the envelope. He picked up the envelope. It was a plain envelope that had to have been placed up there after they painted the closet subsequent to moving in.

He debated whether he should open it but figured it wouldn't hurt. He thought about what might be inside. Maybe there were tickets to a concert or another event that Ryan was going to surprise him with. Oh, if that was the case, he shouldn't' open it, but what if it wasn't? What if the envelope held pictures that Ryan was saving for some reason? What if they were pictures he didn't want to see or shouldn't see? His imagination was making him very curious so he opened the envelope to see a bank deposit book. He turned it around and read the name on the front cover. It read, "Ryan A. Cavazos." Why did Ryan have his own account? Two years ago they agreed to have one joint account. Why did he decide to open a separate account? More importantly why did he decide to hide it from Matt?

Matt went back to the doorway and listened down the hallway. He could hear Ryan talking with the remaining guests so he knew he wouldn't be disturbed. He closed the door halfway and went back into the bedroom. He decided to look through the book to see if it was an old account but noticed that it was opened last year and contained current year transactions. There were small deposits every two weeks, which must have been portions of his paycheck, and random deposits throughout each month. There were five withdrawals for five thousand dollars each and then one large deposit for thirty-thousand-dollars and a withdrawal for fifty-thousand-dollars. The date on the transaction was three months prior to the day. There were no other entries. "What was all this about?" Matt wondered.

As he considered what Ryan might be hiding, he heard his name.

"Matt? Where are you? Are you coming back to the party or what?"

It was Ryan and he was heading toward the bedroom. Matt quickly put the bank deposit book back in then envelope and placed it on the shelf before Ryan entered.

"What are you doing?" Ryan inquired.

"I was just checking to make sure that nothing was broken. I had a little problem getting it down from the closet," Matt said as he waited for a reaction from Ryan. He didn't get one.

"Well, is it alright?" Ryan asked.

"Yes, I think so." Matt replied.

"Is everything okay, Matt? You look a little white. What's the matter?" asked Ryan.

"It's just that it's been a year since the whole ordeal and I find it hard to really celebrate our daughter's birthday," he said.

"I know. I've been feeling the same way. Even though I didn't know Maureen as long as you did, I liked her and I wish things were different. I wish she was here to hold the baby and was around to share in her life now, but we can't change the past. We can only enjoy the present and that means that we have to accept the things that happened and enjoy our lives. Now, I think we should get back to the party before people begin to wonder what happened to us," Ryan said.

"You're right as usual. Okay, let's get out there before anyone starts to suspect anything. We wouldn't want that now would we?" toyed Matt.

Ryan gave him a strange look, wondering if there was some type of hidden meaning in what Matt said but shrugged it off.

"Are you coming?" Ryan said heading out of the bedroom.

"Yeah, I'll be there in a minute," Matt answered. He sat down on the bed and worried about what Ryan was mixed up with. Why had he kept this a secret? Hadn't they been through enough? What he really wanted to do was to ask Ryan what hell was going on, but he couldn't do it. They were finally a family. The last year had been extremely trying for them but they had survived and were now enjoying each other and the baby. Matt wasn't about to jeopardize any of it. He didn't know what to do. This was a time when he would turn to Maureen for advice but he couldn't. He missed her so much. He missed having conversations with her and asking her for her advice. He still talked to her however, whenever he looked at her picture sitting on their fireplace mantel. He tried to forget about the conversation they had months before her death. She wasn't herself and he and Ryan weren't acting themselves. It was a bad combination and both he and Ryan regretted so much of what they said.

Matt headed back to the living room, carrying Jacqueline's birthday gift. Matt helped her open the present. It was a big piggy bank that resembled a frog.

"It's just like the one your mommy had when she was growing up," Matt said. "She always loved frogs and collected them throughout her life. I remember this one time we were in seventh grade on a field trip to old town Sacramento. We had a little time as we waited for the bus to pick us up and she came running out of this little store and asked me how much money I had. I told her that I had a dollar and some change and she pleaded with me to give it to her. I said I would but I wanted to know what she was going to buy with it. She was so excited. She told me about this little figurine that she saw and she just had to have it. What could I say? I couldn't tell her no so I gave her the money. She came back with the ugliest looking frog, it was actually cute."

"Well, how do you know that she used to have a piggy bank like this one?" asked his mother.

"I remember going over to her house and she showed me her extensive collection. Everything she had had frogs on it. Her watch, her toothbrush, her water glass, her alarm clock, and her piggy bank all had frogs on them. Everything," Matt remembered.

The party lasted until six o'clock. Jacqueline Marie was exhausted and was lying on the sofa asleep. As Matt looked around the living room, he was overwhelmed with all the gifts. On top of the box where Matt had placed all of her many clothes stood her Pocahontas doll from the movie, the 50th Anniversary Barbie, an exclusive Limited Edition doll adorned in a lovely red gown with golden accents, and Barbie as Dorothy from The Wizard of Oz. Her grandmother was very excited to have found the doll because it was so popular and had sold out quickly. The Wizard of Oz was Matt's mother's favorite movie to which she quickly introduced Jacqueline Marie. Although Grandma's little pumpkin was too young to really understand what was happening in the movie, she enjoyed the displays of many colors and sounds.

That whole night, Matt wanted to confront Ryan. They put the birthday girl to bed, changed into their pajamas and prepared themselves for a good night's sleep after a very long day. Matt didn't speak a word. Ryan didn't say much either. They got into bed.

"Is anything wrong Matt?" Ryan moved closer to Matt and put his hand around him.

"Nothing's the matter. I'm just really tired. Are you okay?" Matt replied.

"I'm fine. I think our little daughter had a great first birthday, don't you?" Ryan sighed. "For the first time, I feel like we are a real family."

Matt turned to look at Ryan.

"You do? I'm glad. Do you really think we can be a family? I mean now that all our troubles are in past? They are in the past right?"

"What do you mean by that? Of course they are. I don't think we can predict that we are going to live life without problems or issues, but as far as I know it, I would say our bad luck has run out and we only have positive things to look forward to now. Stop being such a worry wart!" Ryan comforted Matt and kissed him.

Matt decided to think about his recent discovery and not mention anything about it until he found out more. His focus was on being happy and having a family and he wasn't about to raise issues that might put them at risk.

The next morning, Cassie called Matt.

"So what was wrong with you yesterday?"

"What are you talking about?"

"I'm talking about how preoccupied you were. I could see it on your face Matt," she said.

"I was just trying to make sure that everyone was having a good time and I was thinking about how lucky Ryan and I were."

"Matt, I've known you for quite a while now and I know the difference between your looks of joy and your looks of worry."

"Alright, I give. You win. I guess I can't keep anything from you can I? You remind me so much of Maureen, do you know that?" Matt looked at the picture of him and Mo at the Santa Cruz boardwalk. It was one of those pictures they had taken in the little booth. It was a black and white picture in which Mo was sticking out her tongue and crossing her eyes and Matt was making bug eyes and a pig nose with his index finger holding his nose upright. He chuckled.

"Last night I found a bank deposit book with deposits and withdrawals in it. I think they have something to do with the nurse's death."

"Oh my God, really Matt?" Cassie was surprised not only to hear about this new discovery but to hear Matt suggest that they might have something to do with the murder.

"The dates on the repeated withdrawals ended around the day when a large withdrawal was made. Do you still have that article about that nurse? Do you remember the day she was murdered?"

"I don't have the article anymore but I remember the date. It was December 21. I remember the date because I called my brother that day to wish him a happy birthday and we talked about it."

"I knew it was around there. Can we talk? What are you doing for lunch?" Matt's curiosity grew even stronger.

"I don't have any plans. Let's meet on the corner of Hayes and Cole. I know of a quiet little restaurant we can eat at, okay?" she said.

They met for lunch and hypothesized what all of it meant. Cassie told Matt that she thought that Kathy Davis, the nurse on duty that night, knew something. She knew what really happened to Maureen and because of this she was murdered.

"You know how upset Ryan was with her," she said referring to how Ryan had gotten so irate with Maureen before she delivered the baby.

"If anyone had access to do something that night, it was Ryan," she continued.

"You know Maureen had a condition, why would you think he had anything to do with her death? Besides, he was cleared of any malpractice by the administration and any charges by the police. Do you really think he could have done something to jeopardize his career? Don't you think the police would have discovered something? I just find it so difficult to believe that Ryan had anything to do with her death," Matt said.

"I think somehow he killed her or at least didn't save her life on purpose. Don't you remember the anger he was feeling during the time when you all were arguing?" Cassie asked.

"Everyone gets angry now and then but they don't go out and kill people," Matt replied, "Besides, she was my best friend and he knew how much she meant to me. There's just no way Ryan had anything to do with her death."

"Well, maybe he didn't kill her. Maybe he delayed getting help. I just think he did something. I also I think the nurse saw this and blackmailed Ryan. He was making payments to her and then he paid someone to kill her to stop the blackmailing."

"My God what an imagination you have! You seem to have it all figured out, don't you? Have you thought about the possibility that maybe Ryan is a victim in this? Maybe that nurse was blackmailing him just to get money or to ruin his career for some reason."

"Do you hear what you are saying Matt? You are basically telling me that you do think Ryan had something to do with Kathy Davis' murder."

Matt's face was white. He couldn't argue with Cassie anymore. He didn't want to believe what he was hearing but it did make some sense.

He sat there considering everything that Cassie had dreamt up and the timing of the transactions. He also reflected on Ryan's behavior and the stretch of his mood swings. It explained why Ryan was so tortured until the nurse's death and why after her death, he seemed so relieved. The timing all fit, unfortunately.

"There has to be another answer, Cassie," he said, feeling sick to his stomach.

"You're looking awfully pale Matt," she said, "Are you okay?"

"I don't feel too good," he replied.

"Just take a couple of deep breaths," she told him.

"I don't know what to think now," Matt said, feeling confused.

"Well what are the other possible solutions then?" she said, trying to relieve some of Matt's suffering.

"I don't know that's why I feel so sick. If you're right, I'm not sure what to do," Matt questioned.

"You can either go to the police or you'll have to confront Ryan. I think those are your only two options, you know that don't you?" Cassie held his hand and comforted him.

"I just don't know how I'm going to be able to do either one of those things but I agree. I have to. I have to allow him the opportunity to explain all of this. We could be wrong, you know?" Matt questioned Cassie, hoping she would agree.

When he and Cassie got back from lunch, he phoned Ryan at the hospital.

"There's something I need to talk to you about, Ryan," Matt said calmly.

"What is it?" Ryan asked.

"I know you don't have time now and we really need to discuss this in person, tonight," Matt responded.

"You make it sound serious," Ryan prompted.

"I just know how busy you are at the hospital and this isn't a quick conversation. That's all." Matt wasn't about to give Ryan any clues. He wanted to see his face when he told him.

"I understand. There's something I need to talk to you about, too," Ryan said.

"Okay, then. I guess we'll discuss this later tonight. Do you know what time you'll be home?" asked Matt.

"It shouldn't be too late, probably around six or seven. See you then." Ryan was somewhat quiet and seemed to be in a rush to hang up the phone.

Matt went for a long walk that afternoon, working up the courage for his confrontation with Ryan and formulating the right words for their conversation. When he got home that night he went to the closet and reached for the envelope that held the bank deposit book. It was gone. He couldn't quite reach the back of the closet and looked for the step stool. He found it in the garage and brought it into their bedroom. He looked up in the closet. He took everything down but there was no envelope. He knew he hadn't imagined it. The bank deposit book was going to be the perfect catalyst to begin their conversation but now it was nowhere to be found. He was just going to have to sit down at the table and ask him to deny what he and Cassie had postulated. But what did Ryan have to tell him? Was it time for him to finally confess or would he deny everything, including the existence of the bank deposit book?

CHAPTER 13

"Questions"

The longer Matt waited for Ryan, the more nervous he became. He looked at the clock and ten minutes had passed. He was tired of rehearsing what he was going to say. He started getting sick again and thought for sure he would vomit. "I've got to do something to take my mind off of this," he told himself. He decided to prepare a nice dinner. Any time Matt needed to forget about his problems or to take his mind off of challenges at work, he headed into the kitchen. Creating new dishes and cooking was therapeutic for him. It was a time when he could focus on enriching the recipes with fresh herbs and spices. Of course, the glass of wine he always had while he cooked helped, too.

He fixed a salad that he hadn't made before. It was a recipe he found as he was going through his cookbooks and miscellaneous recipes. It was from Maureen.

"How appropriate!" he thought as he reviewed the ingredients. The recipe called for pears, mandarin oranges, blue cheese, sugared pecans, and lettuce with a raspberry vinaigrette dressing. He checked the pantry to make sure he had the ingredients or at least acceptable substitutes.

After fifteen minutes the salad was ready and it was time for the main course. He was tired of chicken and thought shrimp would be a nice choice. He pulled out a bag of shrimp from the freezer and threw some butter in the skillet. He opened a bottle of white wine and without hesitation, poured himself a drink to settle his nerves. What else could he prepare? He decided to make some linguini with chopped basil and garlic. When Matt cooked, he put garlic in just about everything. Ryan was a bit more reserved with garlic but was equally a good cook. Matt made the pasta dish before and knew it would be delicious with the scampi. As he opened the refrigerator to take out the basil and garlic, he found the large artichokes he had purchased from the farmers market. He checked the clock again. His mind was soon occupied with boiling the pasta and chopping the basil and garlic. As he started steaming the artichokes, he thought he would add green onions to the pasta. He would need a dipping sauce for the artichokes as well so he began making a lemon, garlic, mayonnaise concoction. He spiced it up with a dash of Tabasco sauce. He felt better. Realizing his glass of wine was already empty, he decided to pour himself another but wanted to be clear-headed when Ryan arrived. He needed to be sharp and to express himself clearly. He stopped pouring when his glass was half full.

As he put the final touches on the dishes he'd prepared, he imagined how the conversation was going to go. He was going to ask Ryan about Cassie's theory, making light of it and then he would wait for Ryan to disprove everything. He knew Ryan was going to have an answer for everything and laughed to himself when he thought about how his imagination had run away from him. They would laugh about it, get on with their lives, and forget about the thought of Ryan being involved in any of it.

An hour later, he heard the door open as Ryan arrived. He walked in the door, dropped off his medical bag and walked into the kitchen.

"My God, something smells out of this world!" Ryan said, taking a deep breath and looking over the feast Matt had prepared.

"Everything looks so good. I can't wait to eat. Is everything ready?"

"Yes. Do you want to help me set the table?" Matt knew what he was going to say but had no idea when he was going to say it. He didn't want to bring it up during the meal but didn't know what else to talk about since he couldn't think of anything else except that damned bank deposit book.

As they sat and enjoyed the salad, they talked about how their days had gone and whether there were repeats on television that night. It was all so superficial. They finished the salad and began working on the scampi, pasta, and artichokes. Matt waited for Ryan to start the conversation but knew he should since he had called Ryan and requested that "they talk." Matt took a deep breath, exhaled, and thought, "I can do this."

"Ryan, there's something that I've been meaning to talk to you about. I know that you don't want us harping on the past and you really want us to move forward and be one big happy family, but there are things I need to talk to you about."

"Good. There's something I need to tell you, too," Ryan interrupted.

"It's about Mo's death and the weeks and months that followed." Matt was hesitant to mention Mo's name because he knew what type of reaction it caused with Ryan.

"Matt, we need to talk about that. I realize that we're never going to be able to move beyond this unless you come to terms with it, and you can find it in your heart to forgive and forget," Ryan said.

"I don't know how you expect me to forget anything. It has been one of the most traumatic events of my life. I don't think I'll ever be able to forget it. As far as forgiveness is concerned, I can forgive you for whatever you did."

"What are you talking about? I meant that you could forgive yourself for the way you and I treated Mo just before she died. What do you mean forgive me?" Ryan was calm as he continued eating his dinner.

Matt picked at his pasta and nibbled at the shrimp scampi. He thought by telling Ryan he forgave him, Ryan would be more willing to talk about Maureen's death regardless of his involvement. But now Matt was panicking. The conversation wasn't going in the direction he had planned. This was going to be more difficult than he had imagined.

"I mean that whatever happened that night. Whatever you did or didn't do, I can forgive you. I know you blamed yourself for a while and I just want you to know that I never blamed you. I know that you did everything possible to save the baby and to save Mo, right?"

"Of course," Ryan replied.

"No matter what happened or happens, I will always love you." Matt feared that he was being too evasive.

"I know you love me Matt and I did regret what happened with Mo. I felt horrible for weeks. I still feel horrible, but I can't change anything. It is too late for that. I have come to terms with it and I hope that you can as well. You say you have but I don't think you actually have. I think you still have issues with me. I think you hold me responsible?"

"Ryan, why don't you tell me what happened that night? We've never really talked about it. It might be good for both of us."

Ryan looked at Matt with a puzzled look on his face.

"Why do you want to know what happened that night? We've already discussed this. I told you how she came into the hospital and I told you about the complications she had with the pregnancy. What more do you want to know?" Ryan was noticeably uncomfortable.

Matt realized that the conversation was not going in the direction that he wanted it to go. Ryan didn't appear to be catching on to what he wanted to talk about. Matt took a serious tone and said, "Ryan, I know something else has been going on. I'm no fool. I was hoping you would be open and willing to discuss it with me?"

"I don't think of you as a fool. I would never think that. How can you say such a thing?"

"Don't avoid the issue." Matt could tell Ryan was missing his point and thought maybe he wasn't being clear enough.

"I'm sorry Matt. This is just harder for me to talk about than I anticipated. I never wanted to think about losing you, but I haven't been able to think about anything else. That's why I've been so preoccupied and self-absorbed."

"I'm not talking about you losing me. Don't worry about me. You are not going to lose me. I just want to know the truth, no matter what it is. I just can't stand not knowing," Matt said.

Ryan's expression changed as he looked away.

Matt hoped he got his point across. He could tell by the look on Ryan's face that he was serious now. Was he going to deny any involvement and plead his innocence or was he finally going to confess to everything that he was involved in and Matt would learn the truth about the night that Mo died and how Ryan was involved with the death of that nurse. Matt felt the energy in the room change. He felt warm but it wasn't the affects of the wine.

He knew how the energy between two people changes during a confrontation. He remembered one day in high school when a kid, Charlie, confronted him. Charlie told Matt to stay away from his girlfriend but Matt didn't know what he was talking about. Even in high school, Matt wasn't suspected he was gay but liked hanging out with Charlie's girlfriend, Patty. They had English and Trigonometry together and enjoyed each other's company very much. He and Patty laughed all the time and often had to be separated in class so they wouldn't disturb their classmates. Matt remembered feeling the energy change just before Charlie swung at him. Matt couldn't remember what Charlie said but noticed a change in his demeanor and just before he threw his first punch, Matt felt a warm sensation in between them. Although he knew Ryan was not going to hit him, the energy was similar. He felt awkward and had to say something.

"You'll never lose me, Ryan." Matt's eyes stared into Ryan's and he saw pain for the first time. Ryan looked like he was on the verge of tears. Matt knew that this was difficult for him. "Just tell me what you need to tell me and we can move forward. Can't you see? This is what's been holding us back. We can't move forward."

"Matt, I...I..." Ryan stuttered and looked pale.

"I love you and I will always love you Ryan. Remember that. Now what is it?" Matt could almost hear the words, "I killed that nurse. I am so sorry." But he waited for Ryan to respond. Matt never thought about what he would do after he found out the truth. Would they go to the police? They would have to. What would happen to Ryan? He would lose him no matter what. All of a sudden, Matt felt the color run out of his face. It seemed like forever.

"Matt, I" Ryan paused.

"Yes," Matt pressed.

"I have a brain tumor," Ryan said.

Matt's head was spinning. That's not what he was supposed to say. He was supposed to discuss his involvement in the death of that nurse.

"You what?" Matt tried to reconcile what he heard.

"I've wanted to tell you for the last several months, but I thought there was some hope and that I could beat this thing, but none of the treatments have worked. It's inoperable and my doctor thinks I only have about six months left to live."

"Oh, my God! There must be something else you can try. Tell me this is a bad joke, Ryan! Tell me it is. Tell me there's something else we can do?" Matt sobbed as he ran to the other end of the table and hugged Ryan, the tears flowing.

How could he bring any of this murder theory up to Ryan now? It was so inappropriate. They sat together and cried for what seemed like hours but had only been twenty minutes.

"What are you going to do?" Matt wiped away his tears and thought that what he needed to do was to be strong for Ryan.

"I'm not sure Matt. That's why I'm telling you now. I can't believe this is the end." Tears rolled down Ryan's face.

"It's NOT the end. Not yet. There must be something we can do?" Matt clutched Ryan's hands.

"Well, I don't think I need to work anymore. I mean, why?" Ryan said with a nervous laugh.

Matt hated himself at that moment. He hated himself for ever doubting Ryan and for going along with Cassie's overactive imagination. He hated himself for the things he thought about Ryan. Here he was spending time trying to connect Ryan to the murder of some nurse they didn't even know while Ryan had been fighting for his life. He hated himself for wasting the last several weeks and months with his own distress and fixation of Maureen's death. What he should have been doing was enjoying every minute with Ryan and focusing on their life. He thought about how much time they had left together and became sick with the thought of living his life without Ryan.

It was a very somber night. Matt couldn't sleep and spent the whole evening reliving his and Ryan's conversation. "Brain tumor" was all he heard, over and over. Matt didn't know what to think. As much as he wanted to forget about Cassie's outlandish theory, it did have some merit. There was still the issue with the bank deposit book and Ryan's actions over the last several months. Was it just the brain tumor that had made Ryan act the way he had? He hated himself as those thoughts impeded his brain once again. There were still questions that needed to be answered. Was this karma in action? If Ryan was involved in the nurse's death, what good would it do to bring this up now? He could spend the remaining six months with Ryan or he could push the theory forward and spend the next six months looking at Ryan through a window at the prison. Still, what if he did have something to do with Maureen's death? How could he forgive him? Matt knew he wasn't going to question Ryan again but that wasn't going to stop him from looking into Maureen's death. He owed it to her and if he found that Ryan was involved, he would have to pay and suffer the consequences, even if he did have only six months left to live.

After tossing and turning for most of the evening, Matt finally got up and went into the nursery to look at Jacqueline Marie. She was sleeping so peacefully. How would he be able to tell her that he was responsible for sending Ryan to prison for the remainder of his life? He was exhausted and went into the living room and sat on the sofa. He put his head down and fell asleep. He awoke around three o'clock in the morning to Ryan nudging him.

"Come to bed, honey. I don't want to sleep alone tonight."

"I'm sorry. I didn't mean to fall asleep. I think I was just emotionally beat."

Matt went to bed but couldn't fall back to sleep. He cuddled with Ryan and held him even closer than before, caressing his hair and thinking about the tumor that was inside. All Matt could think about was the fact that he only had six months left with Ryan and how the outcome of their conversation was nothing like he had anticipated. Ryan rolled over and was now facing Matt. He was still asleep. He looked peaceful, just like Jacqueline Marie. Matt looked at him and studied his face. He loved Ryan's nose. It was the perfect nose. He marveled at his lips. Oh, how he loved his lips. Ryan had full, soft lips. He loved kissing him. As he examined him, a strange thought ran through his mind.

Could Ryan have made up the brain tumor? Was it just a distraction or was he telling him the truth. Certainly, he wouldn't make up such a lie. Even if he was involved somehow in the nurse's murder, he wouldn't put Matt through such a traumatic event for nothing. How would he ever be able to explain it if…if…Matt couldn't think about it anymore. Why was he thinking about this at all? Cassie was a bad influence and was making him suspicious of everything. He had to start thinking about the positive things and how he was going to make the next six months the best of his and Ryan's life together. He still couldn't believe he only had another six months with this man lying next to him. Six months was nothing.

The next day, Cassie called.

"I can't really talk now," Matt said as he didn't know how he would explain what had happened. Part of him knew that she would be skeptical and he just wasn't prepared for it. Not today. "I'll call you later if I have time but I have this report that needs to get out and I have meetings this afternoon that I have to prepare for."

"Well, can't you tell me how last night went? What happened? What did Ryan say?"

"He didn't say anything about your little theory. Actually, it didn't go as well as I anticipated. I didn't get any sleep at all and I'm exhausted. I'll have to call you later, okay?" Matt was rushed to get off the phone.

Cassie caught the reference to *her* theory, not *their* theory and knew something hadn't gone well.

Matt didn't have a report due nor did he have meetings in the afternoon, but he just didn't know how to tell her. He thought for sure she would call Ryan a liar and would think that Matt was stupid for believing such a story. After all, it did seem to be coincidental, didn't it?

Two days later, Matt returned Cassie's call. It was seven o'clock at night and he could hear the crickets outside. It was getting cool in the evenings now and Ryan was working his second to last week of work. Matt told Cassie about their conversation and how devastated he felt.

"Matt, I'm so sorry. Is there anything I can do?" Cassie was at a loss for words.

"No. I'm not even sure what I'm going to do, let alone what it is that you can do to help."

"You must be beside yourself. If there is anything I can do to help, just please let me know, okay?"

Matt was surprised that Cassie didn't question him. Maybe it was his paranoia and skepticism that was getting the better of him.

"Matt, I hate to bring this up," she started.

Matt knew what she was going to bring up next.

"What are you going to do, about our theory?" Cassie continued, making sure to mention that it was *their* theory, "Are you going to bother with it now? I don't see what the point would be. If he was involved in the whole mess, does it really matter now? Just keep in mind that you need to be at peace with all of it so follow your instincts. I don't know what I would do!"

"Yeah, I'm not sure what to do. I know I can't bring it up now. The other night I had a thought that maybe he was just lying, but I don't know why he would. I just don't see him making this up, knowing what it would do to me. Besides if it was a lie, what was he going to do in six months?" I also thought that if he had anything to do with the deaths, he might confess on his death bed. Isn't that horrible of me? I can't believe I was thinking about that but you know how in the movies you always see confessions on the character's death bed. I feel just horrible for thinking about it," Matt rambled.

"I think it's natural for you to question it Matt. You still have unanswered questions and it's just your subconscious's way of getting at those answers. I wouldn't worry too much about it. I think you should focus on Ryan now. He needs you. You should follow your gut instinct. It's always led you in the right direction in the past," Cassie said, trying to console Matt.

She knew he was in pain and that he was confused about everything happening to him and to Ryan. She didn't know how he would manage it all. It seemed too much for one person to handle and she felt sorry for him. Every time he tried to take a step forward it seemed like he took two steps back.

❧ ❧ ❧

Four days later, Ryan and Matt spent the night discussing what they would do when Ryan quit the hospital. Matt requested time off and it had been approved. They thought about spending some time traveling with Jacqueline Marie. Ryan was adamant that he wanted to spend time with his daughter.

They talked about visiting Europe again and visiting some of the places where they first fell in love. As they discussed the places they planned to visit, Matt had to remind himself that this was just a vacation. It wasn't a final trip or a goodbye.

Matt desperately tried to hold back the tears, at least in front of Ryan. When alone, he spent most of the time crying, praying, and talking to his father. Matt conversed with his father often, telling him about what was going on with his life or asking him a question or two. At first, Matt thought it was odd that he would know the answer before he finished the question but he became accustomed to it. If there was one thing he was sure of it was that someone was looking out for him. He hoped that that someone was his father. This time was a bit different, however. As he knelt beside his bed, he begged for courage and a sign. If his father couldn't provide him with guidance, he prayed that God would provide him with a guiding light.

That night, he and Ryan shared one of their most intimate nights together. They caressed each other and felt every inch of each other. Their love making lasted for two hours. Even though they were exhausted, they cuddled, massaged each other, and stared into each other's eyes. Matt was bursting on the inside. He wanted to let out his anger and cry but didn't want to ruin the incredibly romantic evening. Besides, there would be time during the day when he could cry. He had it down to a science. He'd take a break at work, rush into the bathroom, make sure that no one else was in any of the stalls, and cry. Sometimes he was in there for fifteen minutes; other times it was a half an hour. He made several trips to the bathroom over the last week and a half to cry. When he got home, he looked at the pictures of him and Ryan and cried every time. He knew he had to stop torturing himself this way but he couldn't stop. As much pain as he felt, he couldn't seem to rid himself of any of it, no matter how many times he wailed. Life was so unfair. All he wanted was a healthy relationship with someone who he loved and who loved him. When Ryan and he decided to have a baby, it seemed like it was his first chance at a real life, a wonderful life. A life that he always wanted but was so afraid would never happen when he realized he was gay. He knew that what he felt for Ryan was rare and would never happen again. All his life he wanted to love someone the way he loved Ryan. Unconditional love was what everyone searched for and he had found it with Ryan. From the moment he first laid eyes on him, he felt a stirring within his heart. He still felt that except it was stronger now. He turned back to look at Ryan who was smiling.

"What are you smiling at?" Matt asked.

"Just how beautiful you are. I wish we could stay here forever. I wish I didn't have to go tomorrow—to work. I've always loved you. You know that, right?"

"Yeah, I know."

"Matt, no matter what happens, promise me that you'll always love me. That you'll never forget me and you'll remember that I loved you more than anything. More than anything else in this world. I'm sorry for everything that's happened in our lives. I just wanted us to have a perfect life. I would have done anything for you. I wanted you to have everything you desired. Everything you dreamed about. My life had no meaning without you. Until I met you, I was wandering aimlessly through life. I didn't feel like I belonged anywhere, with anyone. And then I met you. You changed my life in so many ways for the better. Just remember that I loved you. Promise me you will never forget that!" Ryan's eyes were filled with tears.

"I don't know why you are talking about this now. It's not like we don't have any time together," Matt questioned.

"I just don't want to forget to tell you this, that's all. You know as the tumor grows, I may not have my senses with me and I just want you to know how I feel."

"Don't worry about me. I know how much you love me and I will never forget it. Never!" Matt reassured Ryan. He laid his head down on Ryan's chest and listened to his heart beat. The rhythm of his heart helped him doze off.

The next day, Ryan called Matt at work. It was rare for him to call as his schedule at the hospital was usually so hectic he didn't have time and when he did have any time, he was rushing to get something to eat.

"Hi Ryan. What's wrong?"

"Nothing. I just wanted to tell you I love you. Last night was wonderful. You are so terrific. I can't help thinking about you and how great it was to hold you and talk to you last night. I love you."

"I love you too and last night was incredible."

"Don't forget Matt. What I told you last night. Just don't ever forget it!"

"I told you I wouldn't. What's the matter?" Matt asked.

"Nothing. I just wanted to make sure you knew I was thinking of you. That's all."

"Not as much as I've been thinking of you. I'll see you tonight."

"Oh, I almost forgot. I'm going to be late tonight. They want me to review all my files before I leave and make sure that they are all in order, so I'll probably be really late."

"Can't you bring them home?" Matt questioned.

"All my files? Are you kidding? Do you know how many patients I have? Besides I have to go over them with the chief of staff."

"I guess I wasn't thinking. I'm just going to miss you that's all. Wake me up then when you get home, okay?"

"Alright. Bye. I love you."

"I love you, too," Matt said as he hung up the phone.

He couldn't help think that something was wrong. Ryan never called during the day to tell him that he loved him. He supposed that Ryan was equally as overwhelmed with their night and was overcome with emotion and wanted to talk to him. Matt knew that both of their emotions were running high lately.

It was around three o'clock in the morning when the phone rang.

"Hello," Matt muttered still half-asleep.

"Matthew Tylo?" the voice on the other line asked.

"Yes. Who's this?"

"This is the San Francisco Police Department. I'm Officer Robinson."

"Oh my God! What is it?" Matt struggled as he tried to awaken from his dream-like state.

"You are listed as an emergency contact for Dr. Ryan Cavazos, is this correct?"

"Yes. Why, is there something wrong? Has he been arrested or something?" Matt asked, thinking that Ryan must have confessed and had been arrested for murder. He knew it. Ryan couldn't bring himself to tell him that he had something to do with the nurse's brutal murder but had gone to the police station and turned himself in.

"No sir. I'm sorry to inform you that he's dead," was the response from the officer.

"What? It can't be? You must have the wrong person," Matt screamed, "What happened?"

"Sir, I would rather you come down to the hospital where we can discuss this. I am sorry to say there's been no mistake. The only thing I can tell you is that Dr. Cavazos died from an explosion. I can tell you more when you get here."

Matt's head was spinning. What was the officer talking about? An explosion? How could Ryan have died from an explosion? This wasn't making any sense. After throwing on some clothes, Matt called his next door neighbor and asked her to watch Jacqueline. He was hysterical on the phone with her.

"I can't explain now. I basically don't know anything except that some officer from the San Francisco police department just told me that Ryan was killed in some kind of an explosion. He's got to have the wrong guy but I have to go down there. Can you watch the baby?" Matt asked.

Mrs. Collinsworth was a widow and was always there to help Ryan and Matt when they needed a baby sitter. She was a lively woman in her sixties who lost her husband to cancer five years earlier. She was the first one to welcome Matt and Ryan to the neighborhood and to accept them as a gay couple. At first they thought she wouldn't understand or approve of them but as she said, "I've lived all my life in this city; if I had anything against gays, I would have moved away long ago. I always thought my older brother was gay. You see, he lived a very lonely, insipid life even up to his death. I don't think he was ever able to accept that he was gay or if he did accept it, he wasn't ever able to talk about it with any of his family members."

Mrs. Collinsworth was thrilled when Matt told her about their plans for a baby.

"I think that is wonderful! You two will make the best fathers!" she said ecstatically.

She was the first one to ask if someone was going to throw them a shower and the first one to see the baby when they brought her home. She was always spoiling Jacqueline with little things she picked up when she went out shopping. Sometimes it was a rattle or a stuffed animal, but most of the time it was a cute outfit. Matt frequently stopped by Mrs. Collinsworth's house so she could see the baby, especially when Jacqueline was dressed in one of the outfits that she had given her.

Now however, Matt didn't care what he or the baby was wearing when he rushed out of the house and over to Mrs. Collinsworth. He was surprised that he remembered her diaper bag.

Matt hurried down to the hospital to meet the officer. Matt demanded to see Ryan's body but the police kept avoiding him. Finally he met with Officer Robinson and asked him why he couldn't see Ryan's body.

"I'm going to be blunt with you Mr. Tylo. Dr. Cavazos was in his car when it exploded. His body was not intact, so we can't show you a body."

"Oh, dear God!" Matt's knees buckled and he fell onto the chair. "What happened," he said weakly.

"What we've been able to piece together is that Dr. Cavazos finished his shift and headed to the rooftop where his car was parked. He was inside when it exploded although we aren't sure how the bomb was detonated. That's about all we know. We are still conducting interviews and interrogating people who were working here tonight. The body was burned beyond recognition and as I said, it wasn't intact. Mr. Tylo, do you have any idea who could have done this? Do you know of anyone who wanted to see your partner dead? Do you know of anything that we can look into to help figure out who would have done such a thing?"

"Are you sure it was a bomb?" was all Matt could think of to ask. He couldn't fathom what the Officer was telling him. Matt stalled as he thought about whether he should suggest that it might have something to do with nurse's death. Could it be that whoever killed Kathy Davis was involved in this? Or was Ryan innocent and now just another random victim of a senseless crime?

"We are positive it was a bomb. There's no way anything else would have created such an explosion and damage. We've been able to identify some parts of the bomb. The preliminary report from our bomb squad was that it wasn't a sophisticated bomb. Mr. Tylo, do you have any idea who could have done such a thing?"

"I have no idea. Ryan never mentioned anything about problems with anyone else. I would have known. He would have said something." Matt kept mumbling, thinking that this was a dream he would soon wake up from. He couldn't cry because it wasn't really happening. He just wanted to wake up. Why wasn't he waking up?

"Mr. Tylo? Mr. Tylo?" urged Officer Robinson, "this is Detective Baker. He would like to talk to you now. Would that be alright?"

Officer Robinson turned to Detective Baker and said, "I don't think he's capable of answering any questions right now. He's despondent. Can't this wait until tomorrow?"

"We can't wait. What if he knows something? It is best to start our questioning as soon as possible after the event, you know that. Besides, he doesn't look like he's in any shape to drive home," the detective said.

"Alright. You see if you can get through to him and I'm going to see if I can find someone who might be able to give him a sedative."

Matt sat there rocking in his chair, thinking about Ryan. He was never going to see him again. It was over. Just last night he told him how much he loved him and now he was gone. It seemed like it was just a while ago that he was talking to him on the phone. Matt could still hear his voice. Did he have a premonition that something bad was going to happen? Matt couldn't feel his hands. He couldn't feel his feet. He could hear people talking but couldn't make out a word of what they were saying. He heard Ryan. "I love you. Just remember that I loved you. Promise me you will never forget that!" At that moment, the reality of the situation hit him.

"Tell me it's not true. Please! Tell me Ryan is still alive. I can't live without him. Oh, God. Please." Matt let out a strong aching scream and the tears fell down his cheeks in a constant stream. "He's not dead! He can't be dead! Will someone please tell me he's not dead!! For God's sake, we have a daughter together. He can't leave me! Not now!" He was screaming at this point, "No! No! I have to see him! You have to take me to him now! I have to see him! He's not dead! He can't be dead!" Matt was yelling at the officer and the detective, pleading with them.

As Matt buried his face in his hands, a psychologist witnessed his breakdown and approached the detective.

"Is there something I can do to help?" he said.

The detective turned to the psychologist and answered, "I think he needs something to calm him down. Can you give him something?"

"I'm a psychologist. We aren't allowed to administer drugs. Only a psychiatrist or medical professional can" she said, "let me see if I can get a doctor."

Matt sat in the chair, his mind racing, trying to accept what these people were telling him. He felt anger and hatred as he looked around the room. The people had no idea what he had been through over the last year. They wouldn't be able to fathom the torment he was feeling over losing his best friend and now the love of his life. Matt looked up at the detective. He was an ugly man, void of any sympathy. His face showed scars from acne he probably had during adolescence. He reeked of smoke and his hair looked greasy. He must have been a single man Matt thought and verified by the absence of a wedding ring. All he wanted were answers to his stupid questions but Matt wasn't prepared to talk about anything.

"Leave me the fuck alone," Matt hollered when the detective placed his hand on Matt's shoulder.

"I'm just trying to get to the bottom of this Mr. Tylo," he said with an attitude.

"I don't care what you are trying to do. I don't have any answers for you. I just want to see Ryan," Matt said, feeling more revulsion and hatred but realizing he was misdirecting it at the detective. He was really angry at Ryan for leaving him.

CHAPTER 14

"Answers"

Matt woke up and didn't recognize where he was. He was sitting on an old, brown, leather couch where cuts had been sown in several places. As he tried to shake off the drowsiness of the medication, he heard the door squeak open. The police detective entered the room.

"Mr. Tylo. How are you feeling?"

"What happened? Why do I feel like I've been drugged?"

"We had one of the doctors give you something to calm you down."

"Calm me down? What?" Matt tried to remember what had happened. It all came back to him. Ryan was dead and feeling despair, he started to cry again, "I'm so sorry."

"Please don't apologize. Everyone handles news like this differently. You can't feel bad for the way you reacted. It's natural when you love someone so much to react like that." The detective's words comforted Matt.

He continued, "Mr. Tylo, just before you went out from the medication, you were saying something about 'him.' You said that he had killed her and he must have been responsible for Ryan's death, too. Who is 'he' that you referred to?"

"What?" Matt stalled trying to remember what exactly he had said. He couldn't remember a thing. He decided to tell the detective what he knew. Well, not everything he knew but at least the part that wouldn't implicate Ryan or his involvement in the murder of the nurse.

"I must have been referring to the murder of that nurse that Ryan worked with. Kathy Davis. You see, I think that these two deaths are related somehow. Kathy and Ryan worked together and I think if you find who murdered her, you'll find the person who killed Ryan." Matt couldn't believe the words that flowed from his mouth, "killed Ryan."

"Ryan is dead, isn't he?" Matt asked, hoping that for some reason the detective was going to say that he wasn't. That Matt had dreamed it while he was out.

The detective knelt down beside Matt.

"Yes, he is. I'm very sorry. Now about this guy who killed Kathy Davis. Do you know anything about him? Did Dr. Cavazos mention anything to you? Did he mention who he thought it was? Anything you can remember might help us."

"Ryan never talked about it, but I know he was worried about something. That's all I know."

"How do you know he was worried about something?"

"When you live with someone for so long you know when they're worried. You can see it in their eyes. It's written on their face. I knew Ryan was worried about something but we didn't get a chance to discuss it."

"Okay. Let me give you this. It has my number on it. If you think of anything that might help us find his killer, please give me a call." The detective handed Matt his card. "Is there anyone you would like us to call? Is there someone who can pick you up and take you home?"

Matt's first impulse was to say "Ryan," but he new that was impossible. He felt the tears well up in his eyes but forced them back and took a deep breath as his lip quivered. He let out a big sigh and let his head fall to his lap. "Actually, if I can borrow the phone I would like to call someone. I don't think I can drive."

Matt called Cassie and asked her if she would take him home. He explained to her that Ryan was dead but couldn't believe those words were coming out of his mouth. The next call he made was to his mother. He knew she would want to rush down to the hospital but he told her to meet him at home. He asked her to pick up Jacqueline from Mrs. Collinsworth's house and to make sure that she was safe.

When Cassie walked into the hospital, Matt could tell she was trying to be strong even though he knew she had been crying. She walked towards him and gave him a hug. Matt burst into tears and sobbed on her shoulder.

"I'm so sorry Matt." Cassie squeezed him tighter.

"Oh, Cassie. I just can't believe it. Just when I thought we were making progress, now this. I just feel like my world has been turned upside down again. Will it ever end?" Matt pulled back from her and wiped his eyes.

"Can you take me home? I just want to get out of here. I'll get my car later," he said.

Matt went home and met his mother. His daughter was sitting in her lap.

"Mom, what am I going to do now?"

"You'll get through this Matthew, just like I did when your father died. You can't see it now but you'll survive. Look at your daughter. She's beautiful and she needs you. Don't you ever, ever forget that. That's what you have to keep in mind. You have to be strong for her and for yourself."

"I love you. You always know what to say," Matt concluded.

It had been two days and still no leads. There weren't any eye witnesses and they couldn't trace any fingerprints due to the explosion and fire. They figured out that the bomb had been made out of materials that anyone could have purchased from a local hardware store. "It was by no means a sophisticated bomb," said Detective Baker. There were no suspects in mind.

"Matt, I'm worried about you," his mother said. She was staying with him, cooking for him and looking after Jacqueline.

"Mom, I'm going to be fine. Don't worry about me."

"I can't help it. There's someone out there who killed Ryan. How do you know he won't be coming after you?"

"I don't. I'm sure if the police were worried about anything like that they'd let me know."

"Oh, I wouldn't be too sure of that. If they aren't worried, why did that detective assign officers to watch the house?"

"What?" Matt asked.

"You haven't seen the officers parked across the street? I thought they were obvious," she replied.

"I guess they aren't that obvious or maybe I haven't been very observant lately," Matt confessed.

"Well, the police must think you might be in danger if they sent them to watch the house," she said.

"It's just a precaution, that's all" Matt said, trying to reassure her.

"Well, I think you need to be careful and I think I should take Jacqueline home with me. She'll be safer there."

"Mom, I really don't want to be away from my daughter. Besides, what's she going to think? She probably doesn't even know who her father is anymore."

"She'll be fine and she knows who her father is! What would you do if someone got into the house and something happened to her? How would you feel then?"

"What if something like that doesn't happen?"

"Are you willing to take that chance? You can stay at my house or come over whenever you want for how ever long you want. I just think it would better if she stays at my house. At least until they find the killer."

"Alright." Matt knew better than to argue with his mother. She never took no for an answer. He knew he could have saved himself some time by agreeing to the arrangement earlier.

The funeral for Ryan Anthony Cavazos was on July 12, 1997. His mother and father flew in from Chicago. His sister met them there from New York. They decided to stay in a hotel rather than stay with Matt. They didn't think it was appropriate considering what happened.

"It would be unsettling staying with you without Ryan there," Ryan's mother told Matt, "you understand don't you."

Ryan's mother and Matt got along very well. They were always sharing recipes and Ryan was always bragging to his mom about Matt's cooking. When Ryan first told his mother and father he was gay, they were very upset and didn't approve. They denied it and didn't speak about it. They hoped that it was just a phase Ryan was going through until he moved to San Francisco. They didn't approve of his decision but couldn't argue with him, either. Ryan was very adamant about becoming a doctor, much to the approval of his parents. They knew he was strong-willed and determined. At least he was going to be a doctor, they thought. Ryan was careful mentioning anything about whom he dated or where he went until he met Matt. He couldn't stop talking about Matt. Ryan's parents never really wanted to know or talk about Ryan's dates until they met Matt. They liked Matt. They thought that he was a great influence on Ryan and could tell Matt loved their son very much. It was then that Ryan's relationship with his parents changed for the better. He finally felt like his parents accepted him and were actually proud of him. Before that, his parents would become embarrassed if anyone asked about Ryan, especially if they questioned when he was going to get married. After they met Matt, both Ryan's father and mother were comfortable telling their friends that Ryan was gay, and a doctor.

Although Ryan's parents really liked Matt, they argued with him about where Ryan should be buried. They wanted his body flown back to Chicago where they were to be buried. Matt contended that he and Ryan had discussed their deaths and decided that they wanted to be buried together in San Francisco where they met and felt so comfortable with their lifestyle. Ryan was obstinate about it and insisted that Matt promise him that he would be buried in the bay area, near the city that gave him so much joy. Matt told Ryan's parents that he couldn't think about burying him anywhere other than in San Francisco. Matt told them that he understood their position but that he wanted to follow Ryan's wishes. Ryan's parents knew Matt wouldn't lie about something so serious. Ryan was the love of Matt's life and he wanted to be close to him, even after their lives on earth were complete. His parents finally agreed to bury him in San Francisco. They decided to have a ceremony back in their hometown for the people who would not be able to attend his funeral.

As Matt dressed for the funeral, all he could think about was how quiet the house had gotten. The last four days, he waited for Ryan to come home. This morning he waited for Ryan to ask him what tie he should wear, but he knew he wasn't going to. One night, Matt thought he heard the door and footsteps coming towards his bedroom. His heart rate quickened in anticipation but no one came to the door. He lay there listening but didn't hear anything more. He thought for sure Ryan was on the other side of the door so he rushed out of his bed and pulled the door open. He saw no one and heard nothing. He hated the thought that Ryan was really gone and that he would never see him again. It just didn't seem real.

His mother was there waiting in the living room along with Cassie. Mrs. Collingsworth agreed to watch the baby for the afternoon. Matt didn't think it was a good idea to take the baby to the funeral. He didn't want her subject to death as he had been at an early age.

Matt walked out into the living room.

"Are you ready?" His voice cracked. He tried not to cry but couldn't help it. His lip started to quiver and all it took was a look at his mom for him to break down. "I said I wouldn't cry and here I go already. Please God, let me get through this!" he said as he looked up.

His mom approached him and wiped away the tears.

"No one expects you not to cry, Matt. You can't help but cry. You've been through so much, if you didn't cry, people might think there was something wrong with you. You'll be fine."

They got in the car and headed for the mortuary. It was a brief but touching service and he was surprised by how well he was holding up. He was remarkably strong as he stared at the pictures he had chosen to place atop the casket. Because they obviously couldn't show the body, he knew his friends and Ryan's family would appreciate pictures of Ryan as a child and as an adult. There was a beautiful picture of him and Ryan that was taken during their trip to Venice. They were so happy together. Matt thought about the trip and how much fun they had. He remembered how much Ryan loved Venice and how he couldn't get over how romantic the city was. The thoughts of Ryan smiling and enjoying every minute of their vacation helped him get through the service.

His mother along with Ryan's mother, father, and sister joined him in the limousine that followed the hearse as they drove to the cemetery.

Matt asked the priest for permission to lay a red rose on Ryan's casket when he was finished with the eulogy. Ryan loved roses and Matt wanted to be the last person to touch the casket before it descended into the ground. The priest thought it would be a nice gesture and asked Matt if there was anything he wanted to say after he delivered the eulogy. Matt knew there was no possible way that he would be able to speak to what Ryan meant to him. He knew that every one of their friends was aware of how he felt anyway. The priest told Matt that when he was done with the eulogy he would look at Matt and nod his head. That would be Matt's sign to place the rose on Ryan's casket.

The priest nodded and Matt took the step forward to place the rose on the casket. The shot rang out. Matt remembered hearing screams and people falling to the ground and running for their cars. It was foggy, but Matt could see someone from a distance behind one of the trees. He yelled at the police detective who was also there attending the ceremony.

"I think the shot came from over there." Matt pointed to one of the oak trees about one-hundred and fifty-feet away. The detective pointed to what must have been an undercover policeman and they started running towards the tree. As Matt looked back at the woman in black, he noticed that Cassie, his mother, and Eric were looking back at him.

Cassie screamed, "Oh dear God! Matt!! Matt!!"

He ran to where they were. As he approached them, he couldn't believe his eyes. The woman's hat was off and lying next to it looked like a wig. He approached them and was shocked when he saw the face. Was it his imagination or was this real?

"Oh my God. Oh my God. Ryan!"

What Matt originally thought was a woman was actually Ryan dressed in women's attire. He was barely breathing.

"Matt. I never wanted to hurt you. You know that, don't you?" Ryan said, struggling to get the words out.

"Ryan, be quiet. You need to save your strength."

"It's too late. I know it's too late. I'm sorry."

"Ryan please. Please stop talking. There will be plenty of time to talk. I can't believe you're alive. Please don't die on me. You have to explain all this. Please hold on." Matt turned away for a brief second and yelled, "someone call an ambulance!"

"Matt, listen." Ryan was pale. "You promised me that you would never forget that I loved you and you always said that you would always forgive me. I…I…I'm sorry. I love you." Ryan faded away. His eyes closed.

"Oh no. No!!!!!!" Matt hollered and fell against Ryan. He tried cardio pulmonary resuscitation on him but there was blood everywhere. He kept trying until Ryan's father had to pull him off of Ryan.

"Matt, there's no use. He's gone."

The bullet had pierced his heart and he was dead. Matt stared at his lifeless body and knew he was gone for good this time. The ambulance finally arrived and the attendants were making their way up the sloped hill. Matt's head was really spinning. The questions poured in from Ryan's parents, his sister, Matt's mom, Cassie. He didn't know what to tell them. He knew as much as they did, which was nothing.

After they got home, Matt took sedatives that he had been given and sat on his bed in disbelief.

Matt's mother talked to one of the doctors who was at the funeral and asked him to come to the house to look at Matt. He told her that she should watch him and try to talk to him about everything that happened. It was the quickest path to recovery the doctor told her.

A couple of days had passed and everyone was concerned about Matt. He wasn't eating, shaving, or showering unless someone forced him to. Ryan's parent's stopped by frequently and Matt's mother moved in with him for a while. They were worried that he might try to commit suicide. At least that's what the doctors were concerned with. Not knowing that Matt already had sedatives, Matt's doctor gave his mother a prescription drug that he said would keep him tranquil. His mother didn't want to give it to him, but he insisted that he have his dose. He complained about not sleeping, so she couldn't refuse.

"Have the police found who killed Ryan?" Matt thought for sure the police would be able to capture the person who had fired the lethal shot.

"No. They lost the man at the cemetery and haven't been able to uncover anything." His mom was afraid to deliver this news and watched as Matt's face dropped to the floor.

"I didn't think so," he mumbled.

Matt thought back to Ryan's funeral and how he met several of Ryan's friends, including several other doctors. A couple of nurses and doctors stopped by the house one day to offer their condolences. One of them had an office next door to Ryan.

"I am so sorry Matt," he said.

"Thank you," Matt said trying to remember him, "I'm sorry I can't remember your name."

"That's okay, it's Randolph Jackson. I worked in the office adjacent to Ryan's."

"Oh, that's right. You're a gynecologist, too, right?"

"No, I'm an oncologist."

"Were you the one Ryan was seeing about his brain tumor?"

"What? Ryan had a brain tumor?"

"Well, yes. He said he was seeing a doctor at the hospital who was treating him. He only had six months to live."

"Well." The doctor looked shocked by what Matt was telling him. He fumbled for words to say.

"Um…there are other oncologists. Perhaps he was seeing one of them. I had no idea."

"That's okay. He must have seen another doctor," Matt replied.

❦ ❦ ❦

A couple of days later, Matt was back at the cemetery, standing before Ryan's casket. The moment was surreal. The only difference was that Matt was weak and numb this time. Part of how he felt was due to the tranquilizers but most of it was attributable to the shock of seeing Ryan, watching him die in his arms, and grieving all over again. He didn't feel much of anything. He didn't feel anger or betrayal even though he had a right to do so. He didn't feel sad or suicidal although he knew that's what everyone was thinking. He enjoyed how it felt to be without sensation. It was relaxing.

After the funeral, Matt seemed to be getting better. His mother stayed with him for another month just to make sure. He was seeing a psychiatrist and making progress. After just a couple of weeks of seeing the psychiatrist, he was able to talk about what happened.

"I just wish that I was able to talk to Ryan and find out what all of this meant. I guess I'll never know but the one thing I know is that he loved me. No matter what he did, he loved me. I miss him so much." Matt was able to talk to his mother without crying. He even talked about work. "I can't believe they gave me this time off. Are you sure they were okay with it? They did say that I could have my job back, right?" he asked his mother.

"Yes, son. I had Cassie help me get in contact with your supervisor there. He told me how horrible they felt for what happened and that you could take as much time off as you needed. Of course, I asked them how much time they had in mind and they said that you can take up to three months off. In fact, he called about a week ago and told me that they were hiring a temporary employee to take your place while you were out. That way, your job would be there when you return." His mother told them all she knew and made sure that her only son was taken care of.

The phone rang and his mother jumped up to get it.

"It's for you Matt. It's Doctor Jackson. He says he worked with Ryan at the hospital and met you at the funeral."

"Okay, I'll take it in our, I mean, my bedroom."

His mother hung up the phone when she heard Matt pick up the other line. After ten minutes, Matt walked back into the living room. His face was white as a ghost.

"Matt, what is it now? What's wrong?"

"He said that a couple of months ago, Ryan fainted a couple of times at work and the hospital administration was worried about him. Supposedly Ryan blamed it on stress but they ordered him to see one of the doctors on staff. The doctor he saw ordered a cat scan to rule out anything neurological."

His mother interrupted him, "so what's that have to do with anything now?"

Matt stared at her emotionless.

"Ryan couldn't have had a brain tumor!"

CHAPTER 15

"End of the Beginning"

With everything that had happened, Matt questioned his reality. It had been two months and he still couldn't concentrate on anything except trying to figure out who was responsible for killing Ryan. Who knew what Ryan had been up to? Why did Ryan say he was sorry just before he died? Matt was hoping that Ryan would have stayed alive long enough to tell him everything. At least Matt could have had peace of mind knowing the truth but he didn't know anything more except that Ryan was sorry. Matt felt betrayed and angry that he had been taken for a fool. Although he still loved Ryan he hated the thoughts that flooded his mind. Was he sorry that he lied about his tumor? And why did he lie about his tumor?

Out of his anger, he became determined to find out everything about Ryan, including his murderer. If he didn't know any better, he would think it was Maureen seeking revenge or something like that, but he knew she wasn't alive. He attended her funeral, he saw her in the casket. He felt as if he was losing his mind. He sat in his room thinking about all that had happened and what he could do. The only thing he could think about was discovering the truth. He was confused and exhausted from sleepless nights. Maybe the police couldn't figure anything out because they didn't know as much as Matt. He thought about going to the police with his and Cassie's theory but talked himself out of it. What if they were wrong? He might create more trouble and heartache for Ryan's parents than needed. He decided he was going to do his own investigation and find out as much as he could.

Later that day, Matt headed to the hospital to see the administrator. He thought for sure he would be able to provide him with answers. He waited for almost thirty minutes thinking about what he was going to ask him while the administrator was on a conference call. He had to be careful not to suggest any wrongdoing. He knew that if he did, the administrator would clam up and ask him to leave. The administrator was an older, bald-headed man who didn't like to smile or laugh. He frequently looked out his window to avoid eye contact with Matt. Although he lacked social skills, he was very articulate and conveyed authority. Matt remembered Ryan telling him about a disagreement he had with the administrator. One of Ryan's patients had complications during a cesarean section and Ryan wanted to make sure that she was fully recovered before he discharged her. The administrator demanded that Ryan discharge her because she didn't need to stay there and "take up space." They argued until Ryan finally said he would discharge her but he didn't. When the administrator found out, he was furious and ordered Ryan to his office immediately. However, Ryan couldn't make it to his office because his patient was bleeding internally and had to be rushed into the operating room. Because Ryan was so diligent, he was able to save her life. Ryan was furious when the administrator refused to apologize or to state that he could have been wrong. Ryan detested him and now Matt was trying to get information from him. He was careful with the words he chose and proceeded to ask him about the night that his best friend died. Matt couldn't tell if the administrator wasn't being cooperative because he didn't like the fact that he was gay and was Ryan's lover or whether that was just his demeanor. Whatever, the reason, Matt didn't get anywhere with him and didn't learn anything more than when he had stepped into his office.

Before leaving the hospital, Matt thought he would visit Ryan's office and his assistant, Betty. Betty was an older woman who adored Ryan and loved working for him. After ten years of nursing, she wanted a job with less responsibility and craved something that would be more rewarding and enjoyable. She found her ideal job when she met Ryan and starting helping him with his practice. If anyone could help Matt, Betty was the one person who would do all she could.

Betty made some calls and found out that there were two nurses who assisted Ryan and the surgeon the night Maureen went into the emergency room. Of course, Matt knew one of them was Kathy Davis who was now dead. Betty told him about the other nurse but couldn't access any information about her in their system.

"That's odd," she said as she looked on her computer screen, "she's not listed in the directory. Maybe she's moved to another hospital."

Matt left the office and headed to the nurse's station in the emergency room, where Betty said he might have luck getting more information on the nurse, Vanessa Mohr. As he got off the elevator Matt saw the administrator and turned away. Matt knew if the administrator saw him still in the hospital he would probably ask him to leave. Matt waited until he saw him depart and headed to the front desk.

Representing himself as an old schoolmate of Vanessa's, he found out that she abruptly quit after the death of Kathy Davis. He also found out that she had moved to Australia.

"That's kind of a drastic change, isn't it?" Matt inquired to one of her colleagues.

"Yes, but she didn't move right away. I think she went to live with her folks back in Georgia for a while before heading to Sydney. I remember her saying that if she was going to live anywhere else besides San Francisco, it would be Sydney. I guess she just decided to follow her dream."

"Didn't anyone think it was weird when she quit all of a sudden?" Matt asked.

"Oh yes but she and Kathy were close and I think her death just spooked her a little. You see, she was living out here all by herself, but I guess you know that," her colleague replied.

"Oh, of course," Matt said, continuing his ruse, "I didn't find out she was here at this hospital until recently though."

Matt tried to get out more information but they didn't know much else. He was able to get her parent's number in Georgia. Vanessa had phoned one of the nurses after she moved and gave her the number but promised her not to give it out. Why she was giving Matt the number, he couldn't figure out except that he thought she was somewhat attracted to him.

"Whatever you do, don't tell her I gave you the number," she said as she laughed and then winked.

"Don't worry, I'll be very discreet," Matt reassured her.

Later that day, Matt made the call and continuing the schoolmate pretense, told her parents that he was going to Sydney on vacation and he knew she was there but didn't have her new contact information. Vanessa's parents were happy to help him out and told him it would do her good to see an old friend from school.

Matt was excited. He was finally going to be able to find out more about the night Maureen died and the extent of Ryan's involvement with Kathy Davis. He decided that he wouldn't tell anyone the truth except that he was going to take a vacation. He had one more month before he needed to get back to work and needed to do everything possible for his own sake and that of his daughter's. It would also be good to get away from San Francisco and all the pain and heartache. He asked his mother to watch after Jacqueline Marie while he sorted out everything and tried to find a way to forgive, forget, and appreciate what he had. He didn't feel bad lying to her because part of it was true. He needed to visit someplace he hadn't been before that would provide him the serenity he sought. It would still be spring in Sydney, just before the summer so it wouldn't be too warm. The more he thought about a trip to Australia, the more he got excited. He couldn't wait. He struggled with leaving his daughter behind, but he didn't know what else to do. He had to know the truth. He owed it to himself, to his daughter, to Ryan, and to Maureen.

※ ※ ※

It was September 28, 1997 and Matt kissed his little girl goodbye. He hugged his mother as if it was the last hug he would ever give. She wept and wouldn't let go of her only son.

"Why are you crying so hard," Matt asked as the tears also fell down his cheeks.

"Just promise me that you'll be careful. Promise me!" she cried.

"I will. You know I always am. What is this really about?" He wiped his cheeks and tried to regain some composure for her sake.

"I'm just worried about you. I've seen the look on your face for the past several months and I know you are in pain. It's the same pain I felt when your father died. You feel like you are on empty, that your gut has an enormous hole in it and it's all you can do to make it from day to day." His mother tried to explain, letting him know that she knew what he was going through.

"That's true mom, but it's just a little different. Someone didn't kill dad. He died from a natural disaster. And he didn't spin a web of lies that made you distrust everything, did he?" Matt said.

His mother wiped away her tears and stroked his hair.

"I just feel like something bad is going to happen. Maybe it's just because Australia seems so far away, but I just don't have a good feeling about this."

"You're worried for nothing. What could possibly happen to me all the way over there? I'm going to be fine. I just need some time to process everything that happened. To forgive Ryan and to remember how much love we felt for each other. I can't do that here. There's too much pain associated with him. I know that everything he did was because he loved me. I know that. I just can't forgive him and I really, really want to. I can't and I won't go on hating him for the rest of my life. I just can't do that. You understand, don't you?" He comforted her.

"Yes. I do understand. Just be careful!" She hugged him again but this time less tears fell.

"I will. I'll call you when I get there." Matt kissed and hugged Jacqueline Marie and grabbed his bags. He headed downstairs to catch the taxi which signified the first step in his liberation from his past.

Although Matt wasn't looking forward to the fourteen hour flight to Sydney, he was excited to be alone. He needed the time to plan his approach and what he was going to say to Vanessa Mohr when he met her. He spent the plane ride thinking about Maureen and whether there was any wrongdoing. He hoped he would find out nothing and that Ryan's story was exactly as it happened. He thought about Ryan and whether he would find anyone like him again. He looked at pictures of his daughter and wept, trying to maintain his composure so other passengers wouldn't see. He tried reading magazines and watching movies but nothing could distract him from his thoughts. He began drinking Cape Cods on the plane and started to relax. He felt the stress in his shoulders begin to melt away. He settled into the cushy, business class seat and fell asleep. Before he knew it, the flight attendants were serving breakfast, preparing everyone for their arrival in Sydney.

After checking into the hotel and talking to the concierge about how to get to the section of town where Vanessa Mohr lived, Matt headed out. The neighborhood where she lived was called Darlinghurst where elegant restaurants and happening nightclubs dominated the area. Matt found the address he'd been given by her mother and walked up to the entry. There was an automated directory from which you could contact any resident. After dialing their number, they would be able to buzz you in. Matt found Vanessa's name and lifted his hand to dial the number. Suddenly he felt nervous. What was he going to say? He had rehearsed so many versions in preparation to this moment that he couldn't remember what his final decision was. If she moved because she feared for her life, he would have to be extremely careful with what he said. He dialed her number and the phone rang. The answering machine picked up and he hung up the receiver. "She must be at work," he thought. Matt didn't realize that it was still early in the day. He was exhausted because of the time change and thought he would head out to one of the beaches that the concierge had recommended. He knew if he went out the beach, he would be able to relax and kill time before he needed to return to Vanessa's place.

He was surprised that he was able to find the concierge's favorite beach. Matt sat on a bench that faced the sun and watched the waves roll in rather violently. The water seemed to stretch out forever as he tried to see land ahead and couldn't. He stared at the rocks that were weather and water beaten and looked liked they had a soft texture to them, rather than jagged rocks that were hard and cold. The colors were a remarkable gray, brown, and black. They looked as if someone had painted them or placed them there rather than being simply a result of nature. There were beautiful lines in them that separated the colors. As he looked beyond the rocks he noticed that the waves, as if all of a sudden, began to swell with ferocity and slam into the rocks. The waves were at least ten feet high and were a very sharp white. They appeared to capture the sun as they pounded the rocks. He noticed that just before the wave hit the rocks a stream of white mist sprayed into the air as if to signal triumph. Further out, he could see a patch of smaller rocks where moss was growing on them. It was a beautiful site. The green also captured the sun that was partially hidden from the clouds. It looked like they had little purple flowers growing on them. As he looked beyond them to the next set of rocks he saw another set of huge waves coming in that crashed into them. It was beautiful. If only he had a camera to capture it. Although the waves seemed to be fierce and hostile, there was something beautiful about it. He was watching nature run its course. There wasn't anything that man had done to create this, to orchestrate it. He was watching one of mother's nature's symphonies. As he admired this he heard a voice.

"Isn't it beautiful to watch?" Matt turned to see from where the voice had originated.

It was a handsome young man, about four or five years younger than Matt. He had dirty blonde hair and a goatee. He was around six feet tall and was somewhat husky. On a second look, Matt realized he wasn't husky but more muscular.

"I think I could sit here and watch these waves forever," he said to the stranger. Matt looked around to see if the stranger was alone.

"You sound American, are you here visiting?" the stranger asked.

"Yes, I am. How about you? You sound American as well?" Matt replied.

"I am but I live here now. I'm an artist and decided to live in Sydney for a while, for inspiration." He looked at the bench that Matt was sitting on and before sitting down, stretched out his hand. "My name is Steven."

"Hi. I'm Matt. It's nice to meet you." Matt moved over to make more room for Steven to sit down.

There was something about Steven that Matt instantly liked. He couldn't place it though. Was it the goatee? No, it was something else. Maybe it was his skin color. It was beautiful. It was a golden tan like those you see on the ads for sunscreen products and it enhanced his sandy brown hair that was highlighted by the sun just so. They talked for almost an hour when Matt decided to leave. The last thing he needed was to get romantically involved with someone, although he hadn't confirmed that Steven was gay.

"Where are you staying?" Steven asked as Matt stood up.

Matt was taken back by his bluntness. He thought about telling him a lie while he pondered the question. He seemed like a nice enough guy so maybe he should tell him the truth. Still, Matt decided to play it safe.

"Why do you ask?"

"I was just wondering because there are so many nice hotels around here, I thought I would offer you some advice if you weren't happy with the place you are staying."

"Oh, I'm very happy with my hotel. It's extremely nice and is just down by the Rocks, close to the Opera House and all the little quaint restaurants." Matt looked back at the waves one last time.

"You must be staying at the Park Hyatt Hotel then. It is lovely."

Matt laughed. "Wow, you're good! Either that or that was just a lucky guess."

"I meet a lot of people and I spend a lot of time touring around this city for inspiration. I think I know every hotel. Besides I'm renting a flat in one of those high rise apartment complexes so I'm not far from there."

"I love the area so far. Oh well, I have to be going. I'll see you. Take care." Matt started to walk away.

"Maybe we'll run into each other or something," Steven replied.

"Yeah, maybe." Matt continued to walk away and was somewhat nervous. Not because the stranger knew where he was staying but because he seemed so nice. Matt wanted to stay a while longer but felt uncomfortable. He didn't want to start something or to lead Steven on, especially if he didn't have any specific intentions. Still, there was something about Steven. He was so easy to talk to. Talking to him was like running into an old friend that you haven't seen in a while. As he walked away, he thought that he should have stayed there a while longer, to really "feel" him out and to confirm that he was gay. Matt knew though that he was there to get his life together and to get answers and that is what he had to focus on.

Later that night, Matt went back to Vanessa's apartment but she didn't pick up the phone. He went out to one of the trendy bars and had a drink. He returned to her place and dialed her number again from the directory. The answering machine picked up again but this time, he left a message.

"Hi Vanessa, this is Matt Tylo. You don't know me but I'm from San Francisco and you used to work with my boyfriend at the hospital, Ryan Calvazos. I'm herein Sydney and I really need to talk to you. I just have some questions that I'm hoping you can answer for me. I'm not here to cause you any harm or anything like that, I just have to talk with you. Can you please contact me at the Park Hyatt down by Sydney Harbour? I would really, really appreciate it. Thank you!"

Matt waited for two days and still hadn't heard back from her. Maybe he had scared her and she ran off again. Maybe the killer had already gotten to her and now the police had his name on her answering machine. His imagination started to run amuck. As he debated on what he should do next, the phone rang. It was Vanessa. She and Matt talked briefly and agreed to meet at the harbor the next day to talk. She told Matt that she wanted to meet in a public place.

"How will I recognize you?" she asked.

"I'll be wearing a red shirt and my black, San Francisco Giants cap," he told her, "how will I recognize you?"

"You won't," she said.

The only thing Matt knew about her was that she was African American and she was scared. He could tell in her voice that she was nervous and annoyed that someone had tracked her down. She made sure to find out if he had been the one who called her parents. She seemed worried that someone else might have called them and knew where she was.

Matt was anxious, worried, nervous, and excited to meet her. He was also starving and decided to try one of the Thai restaurants that the concierge recommended. As he waiting for a table at *Sailor's Thai*, Steven walked in.

"Hi. Matt? Right?" Steven smiled as he saw Matt standing there.

"Right. Steven, wasn't it?" Matt questioned although he knew his name. For some reason Matt couldn't stop thinking about him and how comfortable it had been talking with him.

"Are you eating alone?" Steven asked.

"I was. That is, unless you want to join me," Matt replied.

"That would be great. I'd love to," Steven said.

After they were seated they talked about the foods they liked and decided that they would share a couple of the specials. They discovered that they had similar family backgrounds and were both only children. They spent the next several hours talking about places Matt should visit during his stay. Steven suggested a couple of places that sounded somewhat isolated and serene. Matt avoided the conversation of his daughter and Ryan though. These were topics that were too personal and he didn't want to face them just yet, let alone talk to a stranger about them. It was over the sticky rice and mango that Steven asked Matt if he wanted to meet the next day for lunch.

"Actually, I'd like that but I have plans in the morning. How about later in the day?" Matt proposed.

"That works, too," Steven said.

"Okay, where to do you want to meet?" Matt wondered what they would talk about other than his personal life but decided that hanging out with Steven was better than sitting around the hotel swimming pool feeling lonely. His only concern was that he didn't know how he would feel after his meeting with Vanessa.

Matt awakened early and thought about what he was going to ask Vanessa. Hopefully she had more information than what the authorities were able to uncover, but would it be something he wanted to hear? He didn't want to get carried away with his imagination so he turned on the news. He flipped through the channels until it was time to leave. He walked out of his hotel room toward the elevator and pressed the button. He took the elevator down to the lobby and realized that he had forgotten his cap. He had to have his cap but he worried that he might be late because the elevators were so slow. After rushing out of the elevator and into his room to get his cap, he ran back to the elevator and waited for it to arrive. It finally came and he pressed the lobby button. He looked at his watch. It was 10:55. He only had five minutes to get over to the harbor and knew he would be a bit late. When he arrived, he looked around the dock and noticed a congregation of people looking down at the beach. He couldn't see over the people but heard the police telling them to step back and he could hear the ambulance approaching. He tried to see who it was but couldn't see anything.

"What's going on?" he asked one of the observers.

"I think someone drowned," came the response.

"They found a body floating in the water," another person said.

"Oh, no," Matt thought. He knew in his heart that it was Vanessa. He had unintentionally set her up and now she was dead. How did the killer know they were there? Did he follow them to Australia? How did he know she was going to be at the harbor? He was mortified to think that here was someone else who could have provided him answers and was now dead. He couldn't believe what was happening. Matt moved closer into the crowd to get a better look but couldn't see anything. He pushed his way forward to where he could see the paramedics working on the body. He tried to get a glimpse of the face but couldn't see it. The paramedics continued working on the victim for several more minutes. The crowd was silent and in shock. They were witnessing someone dying right in front of them. Several more minutes passed and the paramedics looked at each other and shook their heads. The woman was dead. A chill ran through Matt's body. How did this happen? He couldn't help feel responsible. As the paramedics moved to place the body on the gurney, Matt caught a quick look at the victim. It was an Asian woman. It wasn't Vanessa after all. He felt relieved and sighed heavily.

Matt waited until noon for Vanessa but she never approached him. He called her and left her a message to see if they could reschedule. He figured that if she was there and saw the chaos, she may have been frightened off. Matt wished he hadn't made plans with Steven because he desperately wanted to talk to Vanessa.

Steven met Matt at the hotel and they headed to the Quay. It was a nice area that had been renovated into little shops and restaurants. There was a small restaurant that had an outside eating area that overlooked the Harbor Bridge and the opera house.

As they sat there and talked about the things Matt was planning to do during the remainder of his trip, Steven asked him, "Why is it that you never talk about your personal life, Matt?"

"We never talk about yours?" Matt replied.

"What do you want to know?" Steven asked.

"I don't know. What do you want to know about mine?"

"Are you seeing anyone? What are you doing here by yourself?" Steven inquired.

"Well, I was in a relationship for close to six years and it just ended. That answers both questions. What about you?" Matt responded.

"I'm pretty much a loner. Since I don't have any family, I just wander around and paint. It's hard to find anyone who would be interested in someone like me," Steven said.

Matt wasn't sure if this was just a statement to provoke a compliment but, in any event, responded, "I think you are very friendly and a really nice guy. Anyone would be happy with you as a boyfriend, I'm sure."

Steven smiled. Matt wasn't sure what to say next. Was Steven waiting for him to ask him out or something? It didn't matter. Matt wasn't about to and was enjoying being friends with him which is what he proceeded to tell him.

"I have to admit, I've been having a really good time with you, too." Steven winked as if to suggest they could take this to the next level.

"Listen Steven, like I said, I really have enjoyed spending time with you but I don't think I want to see you in a romantic way. It hasn't been that long since I lost my boyfriend and I don't think I'm ready for anything like that."

"What do you mean you lost your boyfriend?"

"He died," Matt said as he looked up at Steven's face.

"Oh, I'm sorry. I really am." Steven stared back into Matt's eyes as if to read his mind. This made Matt a little nervous and was the first time that Matt was uncomfortable with Steven. A chill fell down Matt's spine.

A gnat was flying around the table that they were sitting at and decided to land. Just then, Matt slapped at it, landing his hand onto the table, killing the gnat.

"That was so easy for you wasn't it?" Steven snapped with a solemn face.

"What?" asked Matt, puzzled by Steven's demeanor.

"It was easy for you? Easy to kill the gnat. You just took its life without thinking twice."

"Yeah. It was just a bug. It's not like it was any good to anyone" Matt replied sharply.

"So if it isn't any good to anyone, it can die? Is that right? Have I gotten it right?" Steven's voice grew louder.

"What are you talking about? What's the matter? Haven't you ever killed anything before?" Matt was confused by Steven's behavior and was beginning to feel more and more uncomfortable.

Steven could tell that he had made Matt nervous and caught himself.

"Yeah, I guess I was just surprised because it happened so quickly. That's all. I didn't mean to make it a big deal," apologized Steven.

"That's alright. Forget about it" Matt said as he carefully chose his words. Matt wondered if Steven suffered from some type of bi-polar disease or something. It was extremely odd how he changed so quickly and now appeared to be back to his kind self.

"Hey, I have an idea?" Steven suggested, let's take a trip out to the Gap tomorrow to see the lighthouse and the cliffs. If you liked the rocks the other day, you'll love these. They are some of the most magnificent rock formations I've ever seen."

"Uh, I'm not sure that would be such a good idea." Matt wasn't sure that he should spend any more time with Steven. Although he seemed to be fine, Steven's actions reminded Matt of his second boyfriend, Russell and how he acted. Matt wasn't about to get involved with someone like Russell again, even if they were just friends. Was Matt overreacting or was it really no big deal as Steven had mentioned?

"I'm sorry I blew up earlier. I just think that people don't think before they so easily take a life, whether it is killing another human being or a bug. I guess I'm hyper-sensitive to it since I paint life every day and I think there is something beautiful in everything." Steven was pouting with puppy dog eyes. Matt knew it was just a matter of time before Steven would start pleading with him to go.

"It's not just that. I was hoping to meet an acquaintance tomorrow sometime but I haven't heard from her yet. Can we make it later afternoon again? I am anxious to see it and this is my last week here, so why not?" Matt agreed.

That night Matt debated whether to call Vanessa again. He didn't want to be overzealous because she might not respond to him but then again, he needed to talk to her before he left. He picked up the phone and dialed her number. No one was home or at least no one was answering so he left her another message. Matt decided that he would go over to her apartment in the morning and see if she was in. Maybe she would talk to him if it was in person, in public, and in her neighborhood where she was more comfortable. When he arrived he tried to get a hold of her but she didn't respond. He left her another message telling her that he was only going to be there for a few more days and desperately needed to talk to her. He walked across the street and had coffee at a charming little café as he kept an eye on the entrance. He hoped she might walk out of the complex while he was still there. He waited for almost two hours before needing to return to the hotel to meet Steven.

It was late afternoon when Steven showed up to pick up Matt. They headed out to the area called the Gap. From this location, one could see the ships and cliffs on the other side of the water that surrounded the inlet into Sydney. From their side of the cliffs, Matt and Steven could see the Harbor Bridge and downtown Sydney. It was a clear and cool Tuesday afternoon with only three clouds in the sky. It was windy which contributed to the coolness; however it aided in the development of some beautiful waves that crashed onto the shore. As they walked down the path, Matt noticed how secluded they were. And then he realized it was Tuesday and most people were at work. He read the signs along the path that explained the land. There were old bunkers there that had been used by the army during the war and an old lighthouse in the distance that had been re-painted red and white. It didn't appear to be a very tall lighthouse but was very wide.

They spent the day hiking the trails and climbing the rocks. The rocks were beautiful and had a variety of colors and textures. There were even a couple of caves that looked like they continued underneath the cliffs for a long while. Steven suggested crawling back into one of the caves, but Matt said he didn't want to. He didn't want to climb in the cave because they were so dark and cramped looking. Instead of telling Steven the truth, he told him he wanted to enjoy the sun and wouldn't be able to do so if they were in caves.

"Besides," Matt argued, "we don't have much time before the sun is going to set. Maybe we should head back to the car? After all, it's windy and it's probably going to start getting cold."

"Not just yet, Matt." Steven was staring off into the water.

Matt took a seat on a bench that was placed there in honor of one of the lieutenants in the Australian Army. He decided he would watch the sun set as it quickly approached the horizon of the sea.

Steven walked back to where Matt was sitting.

"It seems like it's just us out here. Like the sun is setting for just you and I? Isn't that funny?"

"Why is that funny? I'm sure there are other people out here somewhere?" Matt replied.

"I don't think so. I looked. I think it's just you and I." Steven looked back at the sun that was barely touching the sea.

"So, why don't you tell me just how much you miss Ryan?"

"What? What did you say?" Matt never mentioned Ryan's name. How did Steven know Ryan's name? Where was this coming from?

"Surprised are you? Why don't you tell me what it was like when you found out that the woman who was shot was actually your little beloved Ryan?" Steven stood up and put his hands on Matt's shoulders, facing him.

"What are you talking about? How do you know about that? Who are you?" Matt said, pushing Steven's hands away from his shoulders.

Steven looked Matt squarely in the eye. "You stupid ass fool. I was so worried that you would figure it out. That you might recognize me even after all these years. But you didn't. You are, and have always been, so fucking self-absorbed with your own pathetic life that you can't see beyond it. You can't for one minute think about how others feel? Can you? As a matter of fact you have to run all the way to Sydney, Australia so you can get away from things? Poor little baby! For once, why don't you take a little responsibility for your actions and think about how you affected your own fucking life?"

"I don't understand? Who are you? Why are you saying all of this?" Matt was shaking and began to walk backwards up the path to the main path where maybe someone would see him.

Steven pulled out a gun and pointed it at Matt. "If I were you, I wouldn't take another step. I already told you we are the only ones out here. Don't you think I'm smarter than that? Don't you think I'd make sure of that? You never gave us any credit. You pretended to be such a good friend to my sister and then you killed her. You ruthless bastard. I should just kill you here and now."

"Billy? Oh my God! Billy. Is, is that really you?" Matt stuttered. He hadn't seen Billy since he they were children.

"You weren't at Mo's funeral? Where were you?"

"I was in prison. It was supposed to be a short little vacation for me for armed robbery but lasted for five years. When I heard about my sister's death, you don't know how I wanted to be there for her and to find out the truth. They didn't let me out because no one told me. I didn't know about it until a month after she was dead. Do you have any idea what that feels like?"

"I figured someone, like your Aunt or Uncle would have told you," Matt said.

"They didn't. They didn't want to have anything to do with me. They never came and saw me at the prison. They never wrote. They never called. My only connection to life was through Maureen. She wrote me at least once every month, sometimes more. She told me about the contract. I told her then that she was stupid. I told her she just needed to wait for someone who would make her happy and want to have a child with her but she decided to have your baby anyway. And where did it get her? Dead!" Billy had tears in his eyes and his hand that held the gun was shaking.

"Listen, Billy. I didn't have anything to do with it. It was just a complication from the birth. There was nothing anyone could do. She had a tainted heart, that's all."

"Don't tell me about tainted hearts. If anyone had a tainted heart it was your precious Ryan! He was ruthless with no regard for human life. I don't care that he was a doctor. He was evil and he deserved to die."

Matt was afraid to ask him anything about Ryan as he was obviously upset and demented.

"Do I look stupid? Do I?" Billy was shaking the gun at Matt's head now and was extremely irritated.

"No!" Matt said.

"Shut up! I know you and Ryan killed Mo! And you know something? I didn't want to believe it. I really didn't. But the more I thought about it and the longer I sat in that fucking cell night after night thinking about Maureen, I knew something wasn't right. All I could imagine was how alone she must have felt when she died. So when I got out, I figured I'd do a little of my own detective work. I hung around the hospital and watched Ryan. I knew that son-of-a-bitch was up to no good and I proved it! I saw him meet with Kathy Davis. I saw him give her an envelope and I knew something was up. So one night, I followed Ryan to a bar. I sat down next to him, knowing he would never recognize me. I started buying him drinks and he started talking. Telling me how he had done something horrible and asked me if I'd done anything horrible. I told him I had and that I felt for him and wanted to help him. He laughingly asked me if I knew anyone who could be hired to 'take care of his problem'. I told him that I had been in prison and I knew of several people who would love to help. He said he was just joking but a couple of drinks later he was telling me his whole sob story. I remember thinking, 'what an idiot.' Although he didn't tell me everything, he did give me the details on how I was supposed to make sure that Kathy Davis was silenced."

"That's a lie. I don't believe you!" Matt interrupted.

"Believe it sissy boy! Later that week, he paid me twenty-five-thousand-dollars in cash to do the deed. I broke into her place and went into her bedroom. She was sound asleep when I jumped on her. I had the knife to her throat and told her I wanted to know the whole truth and that I wouldn't kill her if she was honest with me. She went on to tell me how Ryan had given Maureen a drug that made her blood vessels expand and that she was the only one who had seen the drug. The other nurses thought it was some type of pain medicine for the labor pains she was feeling. After the birth of the baby and Maureen's death, Kathy confronted Ryan. He denied everything until Kathy asked him where the bottle of the medicine was. He said he didn't know and that it must have been in the operating room but she said it wasn't. She asked him to empty his pockets and when he wouldn't she threatened to go to the hospital administration. She said he told her that he kept it because he wasn't thinking straight and that he had given her the wrong medicine and was trying to cover it up. She knew he was lying and started black mailing him. She was getting paid on a periodic basis to keep her mouth shut. I asked her if that was all she knew and when she said yes, I told her I would make sure that she kept her mouth shut permanently and I cut her throat. I then relished in the idea of stabbing her over and over, the whole time thinking of Ryan. All I could imagine was him lying there taking the blows that I was dishing out to her. You know, I remember it being so quiet when I was killing her. It was odd. There was no one there to help her either, just like my sister. Maureen died on that table because no one said a fucking word. No one came to help her. No one was there and I wasn't going to let that bitch live knowing that she was getting rich off of my sister's death."

Matt was in shock, "So you killed Kathy Davis."

"Hello? I know you were listening? Having a little trouble processing all of this, Mattie?" Billy pushed Matt towards the rocks that led to the end of the cliff.

"After killing that bitch, I decided I had to take out Ryan and then you. Then my life would be complete and I could have the baby, my sister's baby. I followed Ryan for weeks trying to figure out how and when I would kill him. One night I followed him to a gay bar and waited outside. I waited for about two hours and then I saw him come out. He had obviously had one too many drinks and swaggered as he walked down the street. He came across a bum sitting down in front of one of the closed bookstores. He didn't look as scroungy as some of the other bums and when they turned around to walk away, I could see that they were about the same height. In fact, I could barely tell them apart from behind, other than their clothes, that is. I followed them back to the parking garage at the hospital. For the life of me, I couldn't figure out what Ryan was doing. I figured he was going to get off with the bum or something like that until I saw him fidgeting with something under the car. I looked a bit closer and I could see the bum sitting in the driver's seat. When I looked to see what Ryan was doing, I saw him running off down the stairs. Within a couple of minutes, I saw the explosion. I have to hand it to old Ryan. He was a clever mother fucker, but not as clever as me. It took me a while to figure it out but I soon caught on, especially when the newspaper came out. You must have been so distraught, huh? Anyway, I followed him to one of those little hole-in-the-wall motels by the beach. He was in room fourteen. I remember reading the headlines of the paper the next day, 'PROMINENT DOCTOR KILLED IN CAR EXPLOSION.' What a joke! When I read that I thought he had gotten away with it again. I decided to sit there and wait for him to come out. He came out a couple of times, once to go the vending machines and another time to walk across the road to the beach. He sat there, hunched over, crying. I wanted to walk up to him and put a bullet right in his head but something stopped me. I think I was just intrigued by his plan and wanted to find out what was next. Besides, he was so stupid, he didn't even know I was following him. It was the day of the funeral and I couldn't believe my eyes. A woman dressed all in black came out of his hotel room. I had to make sure she came out of his room because I hadn't seen her enter. I then realized it had to be Ryan dressed in drag. He was going to attend his own funeral. That egotistical bastard! That's when the idea to kill him popped in my head. What a better way to die? How cool would it be to die as you watched your own funeral? Now that was just reward if you ask me."

"Why are you telling me this? It doesn't matter anymore. The police will put the pieces together and figure out you're behind all this!" Matt continued walking towards the cliff.

"Right! They haven't figured out a damn thing so far. They didn't even figure out that it wasn't Ryan in the car for Christ's sake. They are never going to be able to pin this on me!" Billy pushed Matt again as the sun was now gone and the moon was lighting their path.

Matt fell down and as Billy leaned down to pick him up, Matt turned around and hit him upside the head with a huge boulder. The gun went flying into the ice plant that outlined the end of the path. Matt started running back to the path screaming, "Help, help me. Is anyone around?"

The wind was strong and he couldn't see anyone in sight. He wasn't even sure if anyone would hear him over the crash of the waves and the howl of the wind. He ran towards the lighthouse thinking he could seek refuge there until he figured out a plan. He could hear the shutters on the windows slamming against the sides of the lighthouse. He climbed the staircase to the top of the lighthouse so he could get an idea of where he was and where he could run. He looked around to see if anyone else was out there and if they were, perhaps he could get their attention. He didn't see anyone but saw a little house that was probably a half a mile away. He looked back to see if he could see Billy somewhere by the cliffs but couldn't see him anywhere. He was thankful for the light of the moon but the clouds were moving in. He knew it would be getting darker and decided to make a run for it.

Just as he started his way down the staircase, he heard footsteps. Someone was coming. Could it be Billy? What if it was someone else? Should he scream out for help? He quietly took steps back to the top of the lighthouse and forced the door open. He heard the footsteps approaching faster. It had to be Billy. Who else would be in such a rush to make it up there? He was outside now at the top of the lighthouse. Where could he hide? It was too far to jump. He would certainly die from the fall. He ran to the other side of the lighthouse to see if there was anything he could use for protection. The railing was weak and he was able to pull away a two-by-four that had rotted from the weather. He looked down. This was even worse. If he were to jump from this side, he would fall directly onto the jagged rocks below. The lighthouse was nestled on the edge of the cliff. He made his way to the door that led to the stairs. He waited. He couldn't hear anything because the wind was so loud and strong.

The door flew open and out came Billy, holding the gun. Matt took a strong swing just as Billy saw the two-by-four and was able to put out his arm to avoid being hit in the head. Billy fell to the ground and the gun flew out of his hand. It skated across the floor to the other side of the lighthouse. When Matt missed Billy's head with the two-by-four, his momentum propelled him to the floor as well. They both stumbled and crawled toward the gun. As Matt reached for the gun, he felt Billy's hands around his ankles, pulling him back. Matt tried to kick his hands off but to no avail. Billy was on top of Matt and punched him in the face. They exchanged blows to their faces when Matt tried for the gun again. This time Billy had his hand on it. Matt quickly grabbed for it, too. They were both holding the gun. Matt tried to stand up. Billy stood up as they struggled for control over the gun. Matt knew the railing from where he had removed the two-by-four was weak. If he could just get Billy over there, he might be able to push him off the lighthouse. Billy tried to throw Matt over the edge while holding onto the gun but Matt pushed Billy back, tripping him. They fell against the lighthouse when the gun went off. Matt felt something wet and warm against his stomach and knew the pain he was feeling meant that he had been shot. Billy pushed himself away from the side of the lighthouse and as they turned and struggled with the gun, it went off again. This time the gun was pointed at Billy's shoulder. As they turned, Matt gained control of the gun and Billy stood there holding his arm as blood seeped through his fingers. Billy fell against the railing. As he heard the snap of the wood, Matt reached out for Billy but it was too late. Billy had already fallen from the lighthouse observation deck down to the rocks below.

🍁 🍁 🍁

Matt finally knew the whole story but would anyone believe him? He hoped that Billy would survive to corroborate the story but he was dead. At least Matt would be able to put the past to rest and to forgive Ryan. He was sure that he was remorseful for killing Maureen, at least he hoped he was. Matt thought about the desperate measures Ryan went through so Matt could have the baby and wondered what he would have done if Billy hadn't killed him. Would he have contacted Matt? Would he have watched over him or would he create another life for himself and never contact him? He didn't have any answers and was tired of questioning Ryan and his motives. The one question he knew the answer to was whether Ryan loved him or not. Matt attempted to stand up and yell out but when he got up onto his knees he felt an agonizing pain in his gut. He looked down only to see that that his shirt was drenched in blood. He looked up and out across the water and passed out.

The next thing he heard was a loud siren. He opened his eyes to see that he was in an ambulance. As he looked around he saw a clear bag of fluid hanging above his head and traced the tube from the bag to his arm. He noticed that another line was going from his chest to a machine that was beeping. He looked over the other side of his body and saw a man sitting next to him. Matt had an oxygen mask on which made it difficult for anyone to hear him. He removed it.

"Where am I?" Matt asked.

"He's awake!" the man seated next to him said and turned to Matt.

"You're on the way to the hospital. I'm Detective Larsen. Can you tell me what happened out there?"

Matt attempted to tell him the whole story but couldn't believe it himself. He was trying to stay alert enough to finish the story. After he concluded, the man placed the oxygen mask back on his mouth and Matt faded out again.

This time, Matt awakened to a large bright light. The depth of the light seemed to go on endlessly. He felt the warmth it provided to his face. It felt nice and it made him feel comfortable. He tried to focus but could barely muster any strength. He thought he heard music but couldn't tell from where it was coming. He heard voices but couldn't make out what they were saying. They seemed to be whispering. He looked away from the light and saw a surgeon. Was it Ryan?

"Take off your mask," he thought. He wanted to see Ryan's face again. He smiled and closed his eyes.

As Matt regained consciousness, he saw a man sitting in a chair by his bed. The man approached him.

"Mr. Tylo? Mr. Tylo, can you hear me?" he asked.

Matt attempted to answer but nothing came out of his mouth.

"Nurse, nurse," the man yelled, looking out the door.

A nurse came rushing in and looked at the machinery to which Matt was attached.

"I've got to ask him some questions. Can I do that now?" the man asked the nurse.

"Yes but you'll have to be brief. He needs his rest. I'll give you ten minutes, and nothing more," she insisted.

"That's fine. Cheers," he said as the nurse left the room.

Matt cleared his throat and tried to speak again, "Where am I?"

"You are in the hospital. You just got out of the operating room. Do you know who you are?"

"Yes," Matt replied, "Matt Tylo. Who are you?"

"I'm Detective Larsen. I was in the ambulance with you. Do you remember me?

"Oh, yes. I thought that was a dream," Matt said half-dazed.

"No, that was real. Can I ask you some questions about your story sir?" the detective asked.

"Sure," Matt answered.

The detective went on to reiterate the story Matt had told him in the ambulance, making sure Matt hadn't left anything out.

"Are you sure this is exactly as it happened?"

"Yes. Why? Don't you believe me?" Matt questioned.

"Oh, it's not that. It's just that I want to make sure we have all the details and that the facts are correct."

"Well, that's what happened," Matt said.

There was a knock on the door and an officer entered the room.

"Detective, can I speak with you, privately?"

The detective walked toward the door where he and the officer began whispering. Matt tried to make out what they were saying but couldn't understand a word. Their faces looked puzzled as they continued to whisper. The officer shrugged his shoulders and walked out of the room.

"What did he say, what did he find out?" Matt pleaded.

The detective turned to Matt and said, "They didn't find a body."

"What??? I'm telling you the truth. He's out there then. He's out there!" Matt exclaimed.

The monitor began to beep with a flurry as Matt struggled to understand how they couldn't have found Billy's body by now. He questioned his reality. Had this all been a dream like when he saw Ryan? It couldn't have been. Why was he in the hospital then? His thought process halted when the detective spoke again.

"Just calm down, Mr. Tylo. There's no way he could have survived that fall. If he's out there, I'm sure they will find him."

"What do you mean, if?"

"I'm just simply saying that his body could have been swept out to sea. That's all. It may take us a while to find a body, if ever."

❦ ❦ ❦

Matt stayed in the hospital recuperating for another four days until he was finally able to stand up and walk on his own. His mother wanted to fly to Sydney to be with him but he begged her to stay in San Francisco with Jacqueline. He wanted to make sure that they were both safe, especially since they hadn't found Billy's body. He talked to his mother and cried when he told her everything he had discovered.

"How could I have been so stupid? How could I not see any of it?"

His mom replied, "You are not stupid. None of us would have ever thought that Ryan or Billy was capable of murder. Sometimes we don't know people as well as we think we do. It happens more than you think. There was a story on the news just the other day about a husband who killed his children and his wife. Do you think anyone thought he was capable of that? No. Everyone they interviewed said what a great man he was and how he was so kind and devoted. It happens, Matt. Sometimes it just takes one little thing to make people snap and do something that they thought they were incapable of."

"I guess," Matt replied, "but I just feel so dumb for being so naïve. I never thought I could be fooled by anyone. Obviously, I was wrong."

"Matt, the other thing you have to remember is that Ryan loved you very much. He wanted for you two to have the life you dreamed of so much. As odd as it may sound, he did it for you. But it's not your fault. You can't blame yourself. I'm sure he was tormented by what he did and remorseful. I think things got out of control for him and he didn't know how to handle it."

"So am I supposed to just forget about all of it?"

"No. You'll never forget but in time you may choose to forgive him."

"I don't see how that's possible. He killed my best friend."

"I know but you can't forget what he meant to you or the Ryan you came to love for so long before any of this happened."

"I guess so."

"Now when are you coming back home?" she asked.

"The doctor was just in and said that I'm well enough to take the flight home. He's coming back later to release me but I just need a couple of days here in Sydney before I head home. I'll call you when I make my flight arrangements."

Matt wanted at least one day out of the hospital before he had to leave. He was tired of the smells and noises of the hospital and the cold room to which he had grown accustomed. He had finished getting dressed and was waiting for the doctor's visit when there was a knock on his door. The detective entered his room.

"I hear you are leaving us?"

"Yes. I'm actually waiting to be released now. Have you found out anything yet, detective?" Matt asked.

"We actually have, yes. That's why I came over. I thought I would bid you goodbye and tell you that we discovered a body washed up on shore early this morning."

"Is it Billy?"

"We actually couldn't tell. It's going to take the forensics team a while to determine that. The body was severely decomposed and had many scratches and cuts inflicted on it, probably as a result from being pounded against the rocks or perhaps even bitten by a shark."

"Well, I'm not leaving for a couple of days. So can you let me know as soon as you find out anything?"

"I don't think I'll have any more information by the time you leave, but if I do, I'll certainly let you know."

"I hope it's him. I think I'll be able to sleep much better and finally be able to put all this behind me."

"I certainly understand and I'm sure it's him, Mr. Tylo," said the detective as Matt's doctor walked in.

After being released, Matt returned to the Gap where he had met Billy. He contemplated going elsewhere but really liked the view and location and wanted to return. As he looked down the path, he noticed the police tape that now surrounded the lighthouse. Even though he had spent much of his time in the hospital thinking about what Billy had told him, the conversation echoed in his head one more time. He stared out into the water and saw a large rock formation he didn't remember seeing before. He thought about what Alan had shown him. Matt thought about Maureen, Ryan, and Billy. He knew he couldn't completely let go of his feelings for any of them but knew he had to forgive them. He also wanted to decide how he was going to live his life when he returned to the states. He closed his eyes and took a deep breath. The coolness of the ocean breeze entered his lungs. He felt the light mist on his face. He looked up at the sun and felt its warmth. He looked back at the rock formation and exhaled. He did this repetitively until he felt relaxed.

He closed his eyes and pictured Maureen. He couldn't help but feel responsible for her death. He apologized to her as tears fell down his cheeks. The thought of what she went through during delivery made him sick. Had she seen the baby? Did she know how beautiful Jacqueline Marie was? He wanted to trade places with her. He prayed for forgiveness, continuing to weep, until he felt a hand on his shoulder. It startled him. He quickly opened his eyes and turned to see who was there. When he turned around, there was no one in sight. Chills fell down his spine. He closed his eyes again but this time, he felt a warm embrace.

"It's alright. I love you," he heard. Matt continued to sit there cherishing the warmth that was caressing him.

"I love you too, Mo," he said as he slowly opened his eyes and wiped away the tears.

The next day, Matt packed his suitcase for his flight home. He hoped that he would hear from the detective but hadn't. He called him and left his number in San Francisco and urged him to let him know the results of their investigation.

When he arrived at the airport, he felt like a new man. He was now in control of his future and he wasn't about to let anyone take advantage of him again. He was going to build a great life for himself and his daughter. Jacqueline Marie would know how wonderful her mother was and just how special she was to Matt.

As he handed his ticket to the boarding agent, he saw a gentleman ahead of him who, from behind, looked just like Ryan. He rushed forward to get a closer look. His heart was pounding. Even though he knew it couldn't be Ryan, he couldn't help but stare and wanted to know what his face looked like. As he approached the end of the jet way, he lost sight of the man. Matt boarded the plane and greeted the flight attendants. They directed him to his seat. He looked around but didn't see the man who resembled Ryan. Matt looked further down the isle into the economy section of the plane. There weren't many people in the section yet because they were only boarding business class. The next thing Matt heard was "excuse me."

He turned around.

Matt laughed. It was the man he was following.

"Oh, I'm sorry. Let me get out of your way," Matt said.

The man didn't resemble Ryan at all. His face was ghostly white and he had a moustache like Magnum, P.I. Matt chuckled to himself and settled into his seat.

As the plane filled up, he noticed a couple sitting with their little daughter. She was about six-months-old. They must have caught Matt staring at them.

"Do you have children?" asked the lady.

"Yes. I have a daughter. She's a little over a year old now but it seems like it was just yesterday that she was her age," Matt said, "I miss her so much. I can't wait to get back home to see her. I'm sorry if I was staring."

"That's okay. We understand," said the father, "I do the same thing now."

Matt relaxed in the comfortable leather seat as the plane sped down the runway. He closed his eyes and thought about Jacqueline Marie.

"How nice would it be for her to have a sibling?" he thought.

He made a promise to himself, "If I ever decide to have another baby, I hope it's a girl. Because if it is, I'm going to call her Maureen."

Matt smiled, pulled the blanket up to his chest, sunk into his seat, cuddled his pillow, and fell asleep.

0-595-32513-0

Printed in the United States
24864LVS00004B/346